THE HEART OF A SAVAGE 4

Jibril Williams

Lock Down Publications and Ca$h
Presents
The Heart of a Savage 4
A Novel by *Jibril Williams*

The Heart of a Savage 4

Lock Down Publications
P.O. Box 944
Stockbridge, Ga 30281

Visit our website @
www.lockdownpublications.com

Lock Down Publications
Like our page on Facebook: Lock Down Publications @
www.facebook.com/lockdownpublications.ldp

Book interior design by: **Shawn Walker**
Edited by: **Jill Alicea**

Jibril Williams

Stay Connected with Us!

Text **LOCKDOWN** to 22828 to stay up-to-date with new releases, sneak peaks, contests and more…
Thank you.

Submission Guidelines

Submit the first three chapters of your completed manuscript to ldpsubmissions@gmail.com, subject line: Your book's title. The manuscript must be in a .doc file and sent as an attachment. Document should be in Times New Roman, double spaced and in size 12 font. Also, provide your synopsis and full contact information. If sending multiple submissions, they must each be in a separate email.

Have a story but no way to send it electronically? You can still submit to LDP/Ca$h Presents. Send in the first three chapters, written or typed, of your completed manuscript to:

LDP: Submissions Dept
P.O. Box 944
Stockbridge, Ga 30281

DO NOT send original manuscript. Must be a duplicate.

Provide your synopsis and a cover letter containing your full contact information.

Thanks for considering LDP and Ca$h Presents.

Jibril Williams

Chapter One
Cali. LA.

"Why ya over there so quiet?" Triple G asked his Gang-bangin' Goddess who sat on the passenger side of his triple red Maybach S600. Mimi ignored Triple G's question for a moment as she watched the highway lights of LA float by without a pause. She sat barefooted with her leg crossed left over right. A lot of shit was happening on the West Coast. Muthafuckas was catching cases left and right. And top-ranking blood members was being targeted with Federal indictments. Bitch-made niggas was talking at an all-time high. Spook was getting pressured from the Cartel to murder all loose ends. They was going as far as requesting for the five-star generals down to the three-star generals be murdered. They wanted everyone that had direct information about how the FIVE DEUCE PIRUS inner operation worked be murdered. The Cartel wanted these people to be eradicated immediately. The Feds was too close to bringing the whole operation down. Triple G was a five-star general in the gang's organization, but he also was Spook's best friend from the sandbox. So Triple got no worries that Spook would place him on the spot to be food.

Spook ordered that the whole operation be shut down until further notice, but Triple G was still making moves under the radar. In fact, he just dropped four bricks off to one of his personal buyers that met him at L.A.X.

"You hear a nigga talking to you, Mimi?" Triple G stated, reaching over, touching Mimi mid-thigh. Mimi closed her eyes under Triple G's touch and released a deep breath.

"L.A. is flaming, Triple G! I think it would be wise that we lay low like Spook ordered everyone to do. Let's go on a vacation somewhere, maybe one of them islands we always talked about visiting." Mimi blurred her words out, hoping that Triple G didn't get mad because she didn't feel like fighting him tonight or making him take her concerns as a sign of weakness. Triple G was volleying his eyes back and forth between Mimi and the road. The illumination of the moonlight showed the glint of anger that had crept into Triple G's eyes. His lips sneered.

"What the fuck you scared of? Spook or something? Because that's the wrong nigga for you to be having fear in your heart for." Triple G's voice started to rise a few levels.

Mimi looked at Triple like he was a nigga wearing all blue walking through blood territory. Rage jumped into Mimi eyes.

"There ain't a nigga on this earth that I'm afraid of. You got me fucked up bad, Triple. You talking sideways out the neck like a fucking crab or something, nigga!" Mimi said. She immediately uncrossed her legs and pushed her size 8 feet inside her all-red J's. She knew the comment was a major disrespect. Calling a Blood crab was a major disrespect. The word crab was a word to describe those of the Crip gang.

"Bitch, watch ya muthafuckin language when you addressing a nigga of my caliber. Don't make me give you a violation."

That was gang language for when a member of the gang did something to deserve a beat down. Mimi rolled her eyes.

"Triple G, I love you and I respect and honor the codes of this lifestyle we living by. But we are in a relationship so if you put your mutha'fuckin hands on me for speaking my mind, we fighting out this bitch tonight!" Mimi said, tying her shoe laces up, and she started braiding her flaming red Brazilian weave into a thick pony tail. When she finished, she looked at Triple G like, *Nigga, let's work!* Triple G looked at Mimi. She was beautiful when she was mad. The red tattoo ink that inked down her sideburns looked sexy on her skin.

The five-two live wire was something to see. Mimi's volleyball size booty and firm legs kept Triple G in between them. Mimi wasn't large in the breast department. But she had the right size breasts that you could get full off of. Even though the light-skinned tattooed gang-banger was a gangsta God work of art, Mimi wasn't your average chick. She was addicted to spilling niggas' blood, and Triple G loved her to death.

"So you not scared of Spook, then what the fuck with all this shit about us fleeing LA?"

"I wasn't talking about fleeing LA. All I'm saying, Triple G, let's lay low. You acting like you are blind or some shit. The Feds in our city, and they bamming niggas. Niggas that's high up on the chain of command is getting raided. Someone is talking, baby, let's fall back and hit up an island somewhere with clear water and white sand," Mimi suggested.

Triple G looked at Mimi with a stupid ass complacent look on his face. "Mimi, your ass tryna be somewhere cup-caking it with me. A nigga ain't on that shit. A nigga tryna stay in these streets where the action at."

"What the fuck wrong with us spending some down time together?" Mimi questioned.

Before Triple G could respond, Mimi let his ass have it. "You wasn't complaining when you was cup-caking it with the next bitch last month." Hate and fire blazed in the pupils of Mimi's eyes. Triple G frowned at Mimi's accusation.

"I thought we wasn't going to talk about that shit no more," Triple complained. He had yet to tell Mimi where he disappeared to for two weeks. He wasn't laid up with the next bitch but he couldn't bring himself to tell Mimi where he really was at. So he just let her assume that he was with the next bitch. It took him a lot of begging and pleadings to get Mimi to come back home. After Triple G disappeared, Mimi got tired of waiting on him so she disappeared too. When Triple G finally came home, he came home to no Mimi.

"Come on, Mimi, I thought we was over that shit. I see that shit been stewing on ya brain and you been waiting to use that shit on me like a weapon!" Triple G stated, looking from the road to Mimi and back to the road. Mimi didn't respond; she just kept looking at Triple with a crazy look on her face. Triple was stressing her the fuck out. She needed a blunt.

"I think that we should lay low and continue to get this bread." Triple G's phone rang through the speakers of the Maybach, interrupting his conversation with Mimi. He hit the talk button on the steering wheel, and Mimi fired up some Kush that smelled fruity. He already knew who it was on the phone by the car dash board displaying the caller's name. "Talk to me, blood."

"Blood, shit all bad on his end of the gang. The nigga Boot got slump by twelve, shit been on all the news channels!" the caller stated with sadness in his voice over the loss of his big homie.

"Damn, fool, I'm sorry to hear about the homie. Shit be wild as fuck like that at times. When this shit happen?" Triple G questioned the caller. Mimi sat silently smoking and listening to Triple as the caller conversed.

"That shit happen this morning."

"Where the fuck is Whip and how is he taking the loss?" Triple G could care less about Boot or Whip. *Niggas die out here* is the game every day of the week. He was more concerned about the twenty percent of the kickback he was getting from the D.C. Bloods for putting them on the map as an official Blood Gang.

"That nigga off the grind right now, blood. I been calling him but he ain't picking up," the caller stated. "Aye, hold up, the nigga buzzing my line now."

"Alright, find what's going on with blood and get back with me," Triple G said, ending the call by tapping a button on the steering wheel.

"Whip and Boot is the two bloods that you met in DC a few years ago that flew out here that put that work in for you, right?" Mimi asked, mentally trying to place the names with faces in her head.

"Yeah, that's them fools. They got a stronghold in DC. Them boys are serious about growing their bloodline and their money," Triple G said, turning down on their street.

Mimi wasn't going to let Triple G get away with not answering her question about them going to the island and laying low. She jumped right back on topic. "So we laying low until this shit blows over?" she asked. Triple G let out a sigh of annoyance.

"Come on, Mimi. I'm not trying to be laid up. I'm trying to run the bag up!" Triple G stated firmly, pulling into their driveway and looking at Mimi who was staring at him like he was the worse inconsiderate nigga that he was. "If you want to run off somewhere go ahead but I'm in the streets making shit happen," Triple G said, getting out the car before Mimi could protest.

Mimi rolled her eyes but she wasn't gonna let shit go that easily. She reached for the door handle when she saw movement across the street; two figures hopped out the flat bed of a F-150. The assault rifles they were brandishing made Mimi's breath get caught in her throat. Triple G was walking up the walkway to their crib; his back was towards the shooters. Triple G was slipping hard, so Mimi went into action. She grabbed the Mack 12 that was resting on her lap. She hit the horn on the Maybach, alerting Triple G's attention; he spun around just as the shooters started to open fire. Mimi popped out the Maybach like a jack in the box. The only thing different was she wasn't a joker; she was the she devil in the flesh. Her Mack 12 threw up bullets like it was drunk off the Henny. Triple G sprinted to the side of the house for cover. Chunks of the house fixture exploded from the bullets of his assassins. The heat Mimi was pushing towards the shooters kept them knocking holes in Triple G. The shooters had blue bandannas around their face, concealing their identity. Mimi was confused because the Bloods and the Crips had a truce for years now. So why was they here trying to kill Triple G.

Yak! Yak! Yak! Yak! Yak! Yak! The killers swept their weapons across the yard of Triple G and Mimi's home. They wasn't killing nothing but the house and the Maybach S600. Mimi got low and stuck the Mack 12 around the rear of the Maybach, and pulled the trigger blindly. *Rak! Rak! Rak! Rak! Rak! Rak!* Mimi's shots made the shooters backpedal. Mimi's bullets kept them from advancing on Triple G.

Triple G's heart was pumping harder than a nigga in a porn movie. He pulled the .40 from his hip and popped off from the side of the house. *Boom! Boom! Boom! Boom!* The shooters returned fire. The killers' red tracers drew lines in the night lights from the houses on Triple G's street, bringing light to the gun fight. Mimi wasn't glad she was fresh out of bullets, but she was relieved Triple G's gun kept popping off. *Boom! Boom! Boom! Boom!* The shooters jumped back into the flat bed of the F150, still busting shots at Triple G. The driver of the truck sped away. Triple G was hesitant to off the side of the house, but his baby—Mimi—was still out there. He came out with his gun still trained on the street where the shooters had been. Mimi had come from around the Maybach with her empty Mack 12 in her hand. She had hate and tears in her eyes. For a few minutes Triple G thought Mimi was gonna pop a hot one in him.

"Triple G, we laying low whether you like it or not. So get your shit and let's roll!" Mimi ordered.

Chapter Two
Washington, DC

The DC Washington Hospital Center held a horrifying silence. Tata's words were caught in her throat as Whip and her watched two Metropolitan police officers roll Racks out the hospital in a wheelchair. Her hands were bound by a pair of handcuffs. Tata didn't understand what the fuck was going on. They just learned from the media that Boot, Whip's childhood friend, was just murdered by the police after they tried to serve an arrest warrant for Phatmama, his lover and Tata's best friend. Rau'f—her business partner—just called and gave her the heads up that the police wanted her for a string of robberies and murders. Too much shit was happening at once, and Tata wasn't able to process what was going on. One thing for sure was, the Red Bottom Squad had a rat in their ranks. Someone was spilling tea like their tea cup had a hole in the bottom of it.

Tata had to make it to Rauf's jet. She would take him up on his offer to take her to Morocco. Tata's phone vibrated in her hand. Rau'f texted her the airport to where his private jet will be departing from. Whip was sitting stone-faced. The news of losing Boot was devastating. His emotions were brewing like a bad storm; his chest was tight, and tears were formulating in his eyes. The pain was too deep and too raw, so Whip let the tears slip from under the bifocals that covered his face. Tata looked towards the two officers helping Racks in the back seat of the police cruiser. She wondered why there were only two police officers to lock Racks up and not a team of armed agents. Could Racks be the perpetrator that was spilling the beans about their affairs?

"Fuck this shit. I'ma go for Racks," Whip said, breaking his silence and snatching the fo'fifth of his hip. He opened the Porsche door and had one of his Foamposites on the hospital parking lot concrete before Tata reacted.

"No!" she screamed a little too loud, making one of the officers that was helping Racks into the car spin around drawing his Glock. Tata grabbed the arm of Whip's shirt. The officer couldn't see Whip's gun but he still screamed "Freeze!" anyway. The officer shouting drew the attention of the other officer who was securing Racks in the back seat of the cruiser. Tata popped the Porsche truck into reverse and whipped the foreign automobile around in the middle of the parking lot and pushing the truck's gear into drive, causing the truck wheels to burn rubber as they peeled out. The police got on their radios, calling in for backup as they jumped in their cruisers and pursued behind Tata and Whip.

Tata was zipping the truck through the side streets like it was a Go-kart. Whip snatched the red bandana out his back pocket and tied it around his face. He played the side mirror of the truck. He watched the police behind them that was desperately trying to keep up with them, but Whip knew all the police was doing was trying to keep a visual on them until backup comes and box them in somewhere. The police must have had a APB out on Tata's truck; that was the only reason why they got on Tata truck so fast. There was no way the police could have seen the gun in his hand.

"What we doing, baby?" Tata asked, looking for some guidance from her man. Her heart was racing but she knew that she couldn't go back to jail, and that alone made her concentrate harder on losing the police that was behind her.

"We got to make it to the Gardens." The Gardens was a project in Southeast Washington DC known as Potomac Gardens. Whip got on his phone and sent a quick text. Whip rolled the window down and started busting shots at the police. *Bloc-Bloc-Bloc-Bloc!* Whip rode the trigger like a killer that was thirsty for blood. He brought the chrome fo' fifth back in the window with its slide cocked back, showing that the gun was empty.

"Give me your gun!" Whip yelled. The police car that was pursuing them with Racks in the back of it had turned off on a side street, but another police cruiser quickly took its place. Tata
pulled her pink Glock 17 from off the truck's door console and passed it to Whip, the thirty-round clip hanging from the bottom of the handle. Whip tossed the fo'fifth in Tata's lap and stuck the Glock out the window and got to popping: *Bloc-Bloc-Bloc-Bloc-Bloc!* The police cruiser that was viciously trying to keep up with them dropped back a few feet but also returned bundles of bullets of their own. *Boom-Boom-Boom-Boom!* The back windshield of the Porsche spider-webbed, making it hard for Tata to see out of it. Tata side swiped a few cars as she floored it past DC jail on D Street. Whip popped the pink Glock back out the window and squeezed on more shots before the Glock emptied. "Shit! Give me another clip!" Whip frantically demanded.

"In the console!" Tata said, not taking her eyes off the street. Potomac Gardens subway was coming up on her right. A group of police cruisers had joined the chase. Whip ejected the clip and placed it with a fresh one. The clip was a standard one; it only held 16 hollow points. Whip jumped on his phone. "Aye, Slim, I'm a few blocks away, is everything set?" Whip asked. Whip disconnected the call and stuck the Glock out the window and aimed at the police cruiser tires and windshield: *Bloc-Bloc-Bloc!* The impact of Whip's shots caused the police windshield to drop on its driver. Whip didn't want to be too reckless with his shots so he had to make them count. He just needed enough time to make it to the Gardens. It was hard shooting from this awkward position. He stuck the gun out the window again and squeezed off more shots. This time one of this bullets hit the officer driving the police cruiser in the shoulder, causing the officer to swipe against some cars and fishtail out of control, causing the fleet of police cars behind it to crash into the police cruiser. Some of the other cars were able to get around the crash and continue to chase Tata and Whip. The crash gave them enough time that Tata needed to get across Pennsylvania Avenue, heading straight toward Potomac Gardens. The project was coming up on the left.

Whip glanced out the passenger mirror and saw what looked like the whole DC Metro Police Department behind them; they were just making it across Pennsylvania Avenue. "Soon you turn into the project, stop the truck and get out.

Make sure that you stop the right at the threshold of the black gate in the projects."

Tata made a sharp left, did exactly what Whip had ordered her to do. D.C.B Blood gang was waiting with red rags tied around their faces with glass bottles filled with gas in them. Tata grabbed her phone and her purse and exited the truck. Whip was already out the truck before the truck even stopped. Tata followed close behind Whip. She never ran so fast in her life. She looked over her shoulder in time to see one of Whip's people lit the rag that was hanging out the bottle of gas that he held in his hand. He tossed the bottle into Tata's truck and she heard a loud *Whoosh*! Her truck was immediately engulfed in flames. Tata loved that truck but she loved her freedom more, so she wouldn't complain. Whip made it to the back of the building. Once he stepped through the door way and made a right, one of his Blood members was standing there waiting on him. The tall dark-skinned dude that Tata had never seen before gave Whip a white T-shirt which he made Tata put on.

Whip snatched the dude's Nationals cap off his head and placed it on Tata's head and pulled it low over her eyes.

Whip pulled the white T-shirt off that he was wearing and replaced it with a black one. Even though his life was at stake, she still couldn't help but admire Whip's tattoos and muscles. Whip locked B's with the dark-skinned dude and shook it up blood style. Whip led the way out the building. By this time police cars was everywhere, and they were stuck at the project's entrance watching the Porsche truck burn like a barn fire. Whip grabbed the beach cruiser that was leaning against the black gate that surrounded the projects. "Get on!" Whip ordered after mounting the bike.

"Get on where?" Tata mumbled, cutting her eyes at the police presence that was going haywire trying to get into the projects. "Get your ass on the handle bars!" Whip said through clenched teeth. Tata was reluctant to get on the bike's handlebars. It's been years since she had rode a bike in this manner. She knew that her ass was going to be hurting something serious. But she said *fuck it* and sat her big ole butt on the handlebars. Whip pushed off the concrete with his foot and got the bike moving, then he started peddling away like nothing even happened. The police didn't even pay attention to them as they rode right past them, heading towards Potomac Gardens subway station.

Chapter Three

Whip and Tata ditched the beach cruiser on the side of Potomac Gardens subway station. Tata could feel the stiffness at the bottom of her butt from riding on the bike handlebars. Whip made a quick call. Tata could hear everything that he was saying to the person on the other end of the phone, but the jest of the conversation was that they needed a ride to Baltimore International Airport. Tata's main focus was on the heavy police presence down the street from the subway station. There were police attending to the crash that Whip had made happen by shooting out the police cruiser tires, and on the other side of the subway looking across Pennsylvania Avenue the police could be seen in front of the projects where her and Whip made their great escape by setting her Porsche truck ablaze. Seeing all the law enforcements and knowing they all was looking for her gave her goosebumps. Whip grabbed Tata by the hand and rode the excavator down into Potomac subway station. Whip paid for him and Tata's subway fare and went through the turnstile and rode down another set of excavators that released them on the subway platform. The air blowing the DC streets was strangely cold to Tata; she instantly began to slightly tremble. She was fighting not to draw her arms in her shirt to fight off the chills she was having. Whip leaned against a column, and Tata snuggled against him to keep warm. Out of the years she had lived in DC she never rode the subway. She always thought that DC subways system was like New York's, all dirty and nasty looking, but DC subway system was surprising clean and well lit.

"When we get to Minnesota Avenue subway station, somebody going to be there to pick us up and take us to Baltimore airport."

19

Whip said nothing, looking at Tata. He was scanning the subway. There was a few people on the platform waiting on the train but none of them were paying attention to them. Tata nodded. Her thoughts turned to Phatmama and Racks. Phatmama was her best friend. Her heart was in a vicious turmoil for Phatmama. She never thought that Phatmama's past would come back to haunt her and her sins would be broadcast for the whole world to see them. Tata never thought she would be running for her life. The whole goal when Tata put the Red Bottom Squad together was to hit a few licks, run the bag up and put their money together to go legit and have something for themselves. The group wanted to live life legit without having to depend on the assistance of a nigga. Tata's thoughts then switched to Racks. She was perplexed about how the police was escorting Racks out the hospital. Her escort to jail was light; she only had two police officers taking her to jail. That shit seemed odd to her. She was thinking all the shit that the Red Bottom Squad had done together, that the police were going to display a show of force when bringing them in, just as they did Racks. Tata's bones was telling her that Racks was loyal to the soil. She wondered about Jelli and Billie. Jelli wasn't a member of the Red Bottom Squad any more. She had long since turned her back on her sisters for a nigga. And for Jelli's betrayal Phatmama murdered her nigga—Cain—which made the Red Bottom Squad her arch enemy. Tata wondered: *Was Billie in jail or was she lucky enough to get away.* She pulled her phone out her bag, and Whip grabbed it from her, powered it off and threw it in the trash can that was a few feet away from them. "If they looking for you then you have to assume they are going to be tracking your phone!" Whip said, schooling Tata. She was going to protest, but she thought better of it.

"I need to call Billie," stated Tata.

Whip studied Tata's face intensely. Tata could read resentment in Whip eyes. He pushed his bifocals back on the bridge of his nose and removed the phone from his pocket, giving it to Tata. She immediately tapped Billie's number on the keypad. The phone rang in Tata's ear three times before Billie's Southern accent hit Tata's ears. "Hello."

"Billie Mami, where you at?" Tata questioned in a panic-stricken voice.

"Tata, why you calling me from the strange number? Is this your new line or something?" Billie asked.

"I'm calling from Whip phone. Where you at?" Tata asked again.

"I'm at home. Stick slayed the pussy last night. I just woke up trying to get the feelings back into my legs," Billie said, giggling and stretching her thick creamy body in her bed. Tata rolled her eyes on the other side of the phone.

"Billie, get the fuck up—Phatmama and Racks in jail," Tata whispered into the phone. You could hear ruffling on the other end of the phone like Billie dropped her phone or something.

"What? For what? Where they got her at? Do she got a bail?" Billie riffled off question after question. You could hear her moving around on the other end of the phone like she was rushing to put on some clothes.

"Turn on the news—that shit all over the news and Boots died too," Tata said, cutting her eye at Whip who was taking note of every word that came out her mouth.

Billie had one leg inside of a pair of pink leggings and the phone pinned to her ear, using her shoulder. "What the fuck is happening, Tata?" Billie slid the leggings over her backside.

"I don't know, girl, but they're looking for me too," Tata replied.

Billie's heart was really racing. "Since I'm talking to you and

21

the feds haven't raided your house, then most likely they not onto you yet. I need some place to go, Billie, until I figure out what's going on and if Phatmama and Racks is all right." Tata couldn't leave Phatmama and her team behind like that. The person who she is wouldn't allow her to flee to Morocco. And on top of everything else, she knew Whip needed her. Tata looked at Whip and he shook his head, by way of saying no, indicating that she's not staying in DC, but she's staying in Morocco. Tata paid him no mind.

"Billie, I'm at Potomac Gardens Subway station. I need you to pick me up at Anderson Road Subway station, that's down the street from you."

"Yeah, I know where it's at. I'll be there. I got a safe place to take you," Billie stated.

"Good. I'm gonna need it," Tata said, ending the call.

***

Jelli's leg frantically bounced up and down. She had the nasty jail phone jammed to her ear. She was mad as fuck. Fate hadn't answered his phone in a week. The last time she spoke with Fate, he assured Jelli that everything was going to be all right. He dropped a hundred grand on her lawyer, then the nigga disappeared after she was officially charged with murdering Diego. Jelli was apprehended during a traffic stop. The police pulled her over. The officer smelt weed and ran her name. Even though weed is legal in DC, it's illegal when you are on federal papers. The officer searched Jelli's Benz truck and found a handgun in her possession. She was arrested, and brought to Correctional Treatment Facility, pending a court date for the gun she was caught with, and violation of probation, a few days later. She was charged with Diego's murder. The gun she was caught with was the same gun she had killed

Diego with. To add to a depressed situation, the clothes she got arrested in had blood splatters of Diego's blood on it. Jelli was interviewed by homicide, and apparently the homicide detectives were good at what they did because they connected the dots and linked Jelli to Diego's murder after his body was found in the alley on Newton Street N.W. Jelli been sitting over CTF for the last sixteen days on a no-bail bond, facing first-degree murder charges. Fate's phone rang ten times before it went to voice mail. Jelli slammed the phone down in frustration and walked to her cell. Most of the inmates looked at Jelli with smirks on their faces as she walked past them. Her thoughts were too preoccupied with being dissatisfied with Fate's action of not answering the phone, that she didn't pay attention to the women's shady looks as she walked past them. Jelli wasn't new to doing time. She kept to herself and stayed in her lane and basically let the women of the unit do them. She walked in her cell, and immediately she knew something was wrong. Her bed was flipped and her locker was slightly left ajar. She glanced over her shoulder and she caught her celly's eye who was playing spades with a group of women who she really didn't care for. Jelli walked and opened her locker, and the heart of a savage woke up in her heart and lit fire in her eyes. Jelli's locker was emptied and bare. She didn't even have a pair of Institution-issued panties in there. All her commissary and hygiene products were gone. All $200 worth. Jelli opened her celly's locker, and her locker still held her belongings. "Oh no, bitch, shit ain't that sweet," Jelli said, grabbing a pair of her celly's socks out the locker. Jelli didn't talk to the girl much, but that didn't give her the right for her broke ass friends to steal from her. Jelli dropped four thick bars of Institution soap in socks, and tied a knot at the base of the sock to secure the soap in place. She tucked the soap sock in her panties, and walked out the cell and called her celly.

"Meeks, let me see you for a minute, boo boo." All the women who were at the table playing spades in the day room turned their heads towards Jelli on hearing her call Meeka's name. Meeka got up with a little funky look on her face. But Jelli didn't give a fuck about all that. Jelli knew from doing time if someone came in and robbed your locker and left your celly's locker untouched, then that meant your celly was behind your shit getting taken, or the perpetrator who did it respected your celly enough not to touch their shit, and that also meant they got permission from your celly to violate the cell.

"What's up, Jelli?" Meeka said with a slight attitude. Meeka was one of the chicks that was chubby in the waist and half cute in the face. She outweighed Jelli by sixty pounds but Jelli wasn't tripping; she had that equalizer stuffed down in her panties.

"Let me holla at you in the cell for a minute. Jelli said, moving to the side so Meeka could walk in first, giving Jelli her back. *A rookie move*, Jelli thought, as she made her move. Jelli pulled the weapon out her panties and soon as Meeka turned around to address Jelli, her face was met with the sock stuffed with soap. It was like getting hit with a brick in her mouth. "Bitch, you gonna steal from me, bitch!" *Whop-whop-whop!* Jelli repeatedly beat Meeka in the head with her jailhouse weapon. Meeka's mouth was bleeding, and Jelli got her good in the eye. Meeka covered up, and Jelli beat her over the back, arms, and legs. *Whop-whop-whop-whop-whop!* Jelli brought the sock down on Meeka.

"Aggghhh, help me!" Meeka yelled out.

"Naw, bitch, don't call for help, where my shit at, bitch!" Jelli yelled and continued to whip Meeka's ass. All the commotion in Jelli's cell brought all the nosy motherfuckers to her door. And when there's nosy bitches, there's always a snitch in the mix. Jelli could hear the C.O.'s behind her yelling and instructing her to put the weapon down. But Jelli blacked out. She kept beating Meeka with the soap sock. When the pepper spray hit her eyes, burning them and her nose, she stopped beating Meeka and fell to her knees where the C.O.'s dragged her out the cell and handcuffed her from the back and escorted her to Seg'. Meeka laid on the cell floor battered and beaten. She desperately needed medical attention.

Jibril Williams

Chapter Four

Billie sat peevish as fuck behind the wheel of her Audi. Tata's news of Phatmama and Racks being arrested had her feeling that twelve was going to bear down on her at any moment. Even though the Audi windows held tint on them, Billie still felt that everyone that came out of Anderson Road subway station could see her sitting behind the wheel of the truck. She checked the time on the truck's dashboard and it read 2:15 p.m. Billie glanced over at Stacks who sat stone-faced texting away on his phone. He was keeping up with the updates concerning Boot's death, and Phatmama and Racks' arrest through social media as well as the local news. While waiting for Tata and Whip, Sticks showed her a clipping of Phatmama being escorted out Boot's crib in handcuffs after Boot and Phatmama tried their damndest to bring hell on earth to DC law enforcements. The news showed authorities bring Boot out the house in a black body bag. Seeing the image brought a dark cloud over Billie which enhanced her peevishness. Sticks was in savage mode, and Billie could feel his energy. "What's your thoughts, Stick?" Billie asked.

"I don't have none," Sticks said coldly and oddly.

Before Billie could respond to Sticks, she saw Tata and Whip emerge from the subway station and making a beeline towards her truck. "There they go," Billie announced, driving Sticks' attention away from his phone.

"Alright, hit me when you get to the spot," Sticks said, kissing Billie on the cheek and climbing out the truck. Tata stopped at the passenger side of Billie's truck and faced Whip.

"I'm gonna call you, Papi, when I get where I'm going, but why don't you come with me though?" Tata stated.

"I wish you would have just gotten on that plane and let me and Sticks figure this shit out."

"The real bitch in me won't let me flee to Africa and leave Phatmama or Racks behind. I'm not that type of bitch, Whip, now why are you not going with me?"

"My fucking day one is laying in the morgue on cold fucking steel. I got to go claim him and bury my nigga. I don't have time to be hiding out with you!" Whip stated harshly with tears in his eyes. He walked off and got in a car that parked next to Billie's truck. She watched as Sticks and Whip pulled out the parking lot. There was so much shit going through her mind about Whip's statement and action. He didn't even kiss her before he walked away, and that alone had her feeling a certain way.

"Come on, Tata, let's go!" Billie yelled, snapping Tata out of her thoughts. Tata sucked her teeth and got into Billie's Audi, and Billie screeched out the parking lot.

***

"Stand and face the camera," the tall female officer stated without a hint of humanity in her voice. Racks forced herself to stand up out the wheelchair she was sitting in and faced the camera. The tall female officer stood behind the camera that rested on a tripod. The officer impatiently tapped her boot on the shiny floor of central cell block. Once Racks was in position, the officer snapped her picture before she ordered Racks to turn to the right and snapped a side profile shot of her. Racks learned that she was charged with killing a police officer at a gas station and for robbing a string of jewelry stores. The DC police was all over her ass. She didn't give a fuck though; she was ready to die. There wasn't anything else to live for. "Alright, let's go!" the officer behind the camera ordered, pointing a finger towards a steel door. Racks was trying to ease back into the wheelchair. "No. I didn't tell ya coochie eating ass to get back in the wheelchair. I said let's go. You didn't need a wheelchair when you murdered Officer Spencer."

Racks looked at the officer with hate and at the very moment Racks wished it was the female officer she had killed. It was obvious that the officer wanted to see her in pain. A few weeks ago Jelli and her goons had caught Racks slipping. She was beaten and raped. The encounter left Racks with a ripped sphincter muscle; nine stitches held her rectum together. Racks was in no condition to be walking but she wouldn't give the officer the satisfaction of seeing her beg to use the wheelchair. Racks sucked it up and pushed through the pain. The officer snickered. "You think you's a tough bitch. They gonna be fucking you with all type of broom stick and mop handles once they get your ass over that jail. Your ass won't make it to trial!" the officer said, opening the door and leading Racks down a corridor. When Racks walked in the holding cell, the officer kicked Racks in the ass. "That's for Officer Spencer, you bull dyke ass bitch!" The officer slammed and secured the door behind Racks and walked away feeling good about getting some retribution for her slain comrade.

Racks fell to the cold dirty floor. Her ass was on fire. Before she could regroup and get to her feet, her name was called. "Racks!" Looking up, she saw Phatmama rushing towards her. Racks was relieved to see her. "Phatmama!" Racks said with a dry mouth.

"Come on, let me help you up!" Phatmama helped her sister-in- arms over to the small steel bench that was bolted to the wall. Racks opted to lay on her side. The pain in her butt was too much for her to sit down on. Phatmama knew the police must've grabbed Racks from the hospital because her and Boot was supposed to have met Racks at Tata's crib when she got discharged from the hospital. "Racks, what the fuck is going on?" Phatmama yammered.

"Your guess is just as good as mine. One thing for sure is we got a rat in our ranks. Someone is working with twelve. Them crackas know way too much. They talking about me killing that police at the gas station." Phatmama wasn't there when that event took place but she had heard about the details through Tata and Zoey. "The only people who were there when that shit happen was Zoey, Tata and Jelli. Zoey is dead so she is not the one that's talking. The mention of Zoey deepened the pain she held in her heart. Phatmama shook her head, taking in the info Racks was dropping on her. "It's nobody but that fraud ass bitch Jelli talking. It's no secret how she feels about me!" Racks said with malice in her voice.

"We got to get to a phone and get word to Tata," Phatmama said.

"Tata already know something is up. Her and Whip was at the hospital trying to pick me up when twelve got their line. Tata took them people on a ride. I was in the back seat of one of the cruisers when the chase started then twelve faded back and brought me here. I heard over the police radio that Tata and Whip got away!" Racks said with a smirk on her face. Phatmama was happy about that but she had to find a way to get in touch with Tata or at least Billie. Boot came to her mind and it dawned on her that Racks didn't know that Boot was dead. Phatmama put her head down and took a deep breath before she relayed the news to Racks.

"Racks, I got something to tell you—" Phatmama paused. "Boot is dead. The police killed him this morning when they came to his crib to arrest me."

The event came back to her like a fifty-foot wave, strong and hard. Tears flooded her eyes. Thinking about the many bullets holes that riddled Boot's body played over and over in her mind like an old black and white movie. This movie played in slow motion, so every detail was very vivid to her. Boot was Phatmama's love and he was gone forever, and the thought of never seeing him again crushed her soul. Racks' mind instantly withdrew from reality. She faced the concrete and focused on a spot that was there, and allowed the hot tears for her comrade to run freely.

Jibril Williams

Chapter Five
The Next Day

Tata and Billie was ducked off in a low-key spot out Laurel, MD. They been up all night smoking and placing calls to different police precincts, trying to find out where the fuck Phatmama and Racks are being held. They learned from the morning news that both of them will be arraigned this morning. The media was eating all the bullshit up about Phatmama being the genital killer. And Racks being a cop killer. What took things to a great height was how they put Phatmama and Racks together being part of the infamous Red Bottom Squad. Tata just shook her head at all the bullshit. It was obvious that someone was flapping their dick suckers in her squad. It couldn't be Phatmama or Racks. Zoey was dead. The only person it could be is Jelli or Billie. Tata looked at Billie who sat Indian style rolling a Backwood. Billie was the last member to join the Red Bottom Squad under Phatmama's request. Her and Phatmama went back into their military days. She didn't know Billie to say what she really would do or wouldn't do. Tata looked at the FN that was sitting next to her new phone. Billie stopped and grabbed it for her on the way to the hideout. She looked back at Billie. She wondered why the police wasn't looking for Billie but was looking for everyone else in the squad. All types of suspicions were running through her head. *Could Billie be the rat? Why haven't the Feds raided her house and why weren't the Feds outside now demanding her to come out with her hands up?* Tata glanced over at Billie before picking the FN up off the table. She stared at the side of Billie's head where she was thinking about placing a bullet. It was always better to be safe than to be sorry. Tata's face flashed across the 50-inch Sony flat screen.

"Providenica Llanos, head leader of the Red Bottom Squad is wanted on several serious charges," the news reporter reported. "Charges are first-degree murder, grand larceny, armed robbery, conspiracy—"

Tata got goosebumps thinking about the time she would be facing if she was convicted of any of the charges they were trying to charge her with. Billie grabbed the remote and elevated the volume on the TV. "There had been reports that the authorities had a slew of evidence on the vicious robbery gang. Tanya Foxx and Rachelle Bank are scheduled to appear in court today at 11:00 a.m. Our sources tell us that there may be more members of the sophisticated gang. If anyone knows the whereabouts of Providenica Llanos, contact the authorities at the number located on the bottom of your TV screen. Do not approach this suspect as she is considered armed and dangerous."

"Damn," Billie yammered, turning the volume back down on the TV. Tata was mad as fuck that twelve were really looking for her. So it really wasn't a coincidence why the police got on her line so quickly. They were already looking for her when they went to snatch Racks up at the hospital.

"We need to get word to Phatmama. We got to let her know that we are here for her and Racks," Billie said, blowing a cloud of smoke in the air. Tata didn't acknowledge her statement, and Billie noticed the atmosphere in the room changed. Billie turned to look at Tata, and for the first time she realized that Tata had picked the FN up off the table. Billie's ocean-blue eyes perforated Tata's brown eyes. Not an ounce of fear appeared in Billie's eyes. Without diverting her eyes from Tata's, Billie began to calmly speak. "Undying loyalty," Billie mumbled through a cloud of smoke. "Undying loyalty is what I stated to you and the Red Bottom Squad the first day the group brought me into their inner circle. The Red Bottom

Squad Motto is: *If one rides, we all roll. If one hesitated, then we all motivate and if one betrays, then God forgives; we don't.* I live by that shit for real, Tata. There's no need to be sitting over there contemplating killing me when I have not betrayed the sisterhood." Billie paused and inhaled on the Backwood before she continued to talk again. "I know that you wondering why the police isn't chasing me or kicking in my door. I'm sitting here trying to figure the same shit out. All I can think of is whoever talking doesn't have enough info on me to give to the police, but I'm sure that twelve will be on me sooner or later. They already reporting there's some other members of the Red Bottom Squad." Tata sat there taking in everything that Billie was saying. She was paying attention to Billie's body language. Her posture stated she was confident in what she was saying. "I know that you are in panic mode and during those times we have the tendency to make some bad decisions. Don't let this be a bad decision that you about to make," Billie calmly stated.

Tata let out a deep breath, not knowing she was holding her breath the entire time. She eased the FN back on the table and whispered the words, "Death Before Dishonor."

"Until the casket drops," Billie replied back, passing the wood to Tata. She wasn't even mad at the way of Tata's line of thinking. If she was in that position, she would definitely be questioning Tata. To ease the tension in the room, Billie changed the subject. "I'm gonna go to Phatmama and Rack's hearing. I'm going to have two of DC's top lawyers to meet me at the court building. I'm gonna drop a bag on them to represent Phatmama and Racks."

"I think that would be a boss move. I got a few dollars at the club in the safe. From my staff at the club. Twelve raided the club looking for me and any merch from any of the heist we pulled off. I don't know if they were able to get in the safe or not," Tata said in between puffs of the wood. "I don't even know if they raided my crib. They shouldn't have though because the apartment is in Whip's name."

"Well, have Whip creep out there and see wassup," Billie said, getting up and heading towards the bathroom to shower and get ready for Phatmama and Racks' court date. She left Tata with her thoughts.

Tata picked up her phone and dialed Whip's number, but it went straight to voicemail. She hadn't spoken to him since he delivered her to Billie. She dialed Rau'f's number and it went to voicemail. She was going to have him use his connects to do a background check on Billie. Rau'f probably was still pissed that she declined to flee the country with him. But abandoning her girls was something she couldn't do. When she talked to Rau'f, he gave her game and conveyed that the best way to help her friends was to get somewhere safe and regroup and strategize the best move for Racks and Phatmama. She would never be any good to them if she were captured along with her friends. Tata understood, but she still declined and stayed in the States. She just hoped now she made the best decision.

Chapter Six

Whip stepped out of Sticks' midnight-black Lexus. His phone vibrated in his hand; it was Tata. He sent her call to voicemail. He didn't want to talk with her at the moment. His mood was the color of Sticks' car: *Black*. The sky lit up with lightning, causing a great rumble of thunder to be heard. A light downpour started to fall from the sky. Sticks exited the car behind Whip. "No. Sticks, fall back. I need to do this by myself, blood," Whip stated over his shoulder.

"Blood, we walking this road together," Sticks replied.

"Fall back! I got this," Whip retorted, pushing his phone in the back pocket of this Louis Vuitton jeans. He pushed his thick bifocals back on the bridge of this nose and stuffed his hands in the front pocket of his jeans. Sticks wanted to badly defy this leader's wishes. He didn't reluctantly get back behind the wheel of his Lex and watch the back of Whip. Sticks' phone chirped and notified him that he had a text. It was Billie telling him her plan to appear at Phatmama and Racks arraignment hearing. He looked at the screen of his phone then back to the back of Whip as he entered the city morgue.

Walking into the morgue, Whip could smell the death that lingered in the air so much that the facility tried so desperately to cover the stench up with disinfectant. But, being so familiar with death and its smells, Whip recognized the odor when he broke the threshold of the morgue.

A knot of hurt and uncertainty formulated in the pit of his stomach. He approached the desk where a plump white woman was sitting behind. She was deep into a game of Sudoku. She hadn't diverted her eyes from the book puzzle to see who had entered into the morgue.

"Excuse me, I'm here to identify my brother's body."

The woman lifted her head from her puzzle and locked eyes on Whip. The thick glasses and the way Whip held his face expressions kind of intimidated her. The man that stood before her gave her the aura that he was a dangerous person.

"Name of deceased and identification please." The woman stumbled with her words.

"Terrance Dixium," Whip said, pushing his ID card to the woman who quickly inspected Whip's ID and passed it back to him. She made a quick call and moments later a tall attractive woman came from out the back wearing a white lab coat. The lab coat bore the name tag *Bones*. Whip found that ironic. Doctor Bones waved her hand for Whip to follow her down a long corridor. Doctor Bones didn't even care to make small talk with Whip; to her it was just another day at the office, and Whip was okay with Doctor Bone's lack of social skills.

The farther they traveled down the corridor, the stronger the
stench of death became. They made a right at the end of the corridor and entered through stainless steel doors. "I have to warn you that what you're about to witness is very graphic," Doctor Bones said over her shoulder. Whip didn't reply; he just followed the woman who stopped in front of a body that was laying on a metal slab with a white sheet covering it. Whip's heart rapidly pounded in his chest; his breathing became rigid. Doctor Bones pulled the sheet back, and Boot laid underneath it. Seeing Boot, Whip's breathing and heart seemed to stop all at once; his legs became weak.

"Is this Terrance Dixium?" Doctor Bones asked.

Whip couldn't answer the doctor. His hearing seemed to stop working. All that seemed to be working at the time was his tears because the salty liquid trickled down from under his bifocals. Whip pulled the sheet down farther on Boot's body.

Doctor Bones grabbed his wrist to try to stop him. Whip snatched his wrist from her grip. The glare he gave her could have stopped the earth from rotating. And that scared the fuck out of Doctor Bones. She took a step back. "Mr. Alexander, is the decease your brother?" Doctor Bones asked. With hesitation Whip nodded. Just to even acknowledge that it was indeed Boot laying across the table hurt him. Whip stepped closer to Boot's cold body and placed his hand on his forehead. The doctor told Whip she'll give him a few minutes alone with Mr. Dixium, and excused herself.

Whip inhaled and exhaled deeply; pain wreak havoc on his heart. Boot's skin felt damp and pasty under his touch. "Look what them crackas done to you, homie!" Whip whispered through tears. He wiped some tears away with the heel of his hand. But the more he wiped the more the river of tears ran freely down his face. Seeing Boot in this state was mentally crushing for Whip. He wanted to kill something or someone. He didn't want Boot's death to be in vain and no one held accountable for it. Right there at that very moment Whip decided that someone would pay for Boot's death, but he just hadn't decided who. Whip used the bottom of his shirt to remove the wetness from his face along with the snot that dripped from his nose. Whip G'ed up and pulled himself together. He leaned over and kissed Boot on the forehead and bumped a blood sign over Boot's chest where his heart was located. "Luv you, my nigga. Rest in Blood!" Whip mumbled as he placed the sheet back over Boot's body and left the morgue.

***

Mimi had her feet planted firmly on the hotel bed. Her small hands were stationed on Triple G's chest. She rode up and down on Triple G's thickness like she was a professional horse jockey. Triple G bit down on his bottom lip as he watched Mimi's love garden eat his snake up and spit it back out more slippery and wet as it was the stroke before. "Hummm, Triple, you all in a bitch stomach. Bae, it's all in my stomach!" Mimi yammered out. Mimi might have been a real live gangsta bitch, but that good D always brought out the soft side out of her. Triple G placed both hands on Mimi's soft backside, a hand on each cheek. He added pleasure by helping Mimi with her thrusts, thrusting her harder into him. You could hear Triple G's toes crack over Mimi's moans and the clapping of their bodies when their sweaty bodies made contact. Mimi's eyes rolled around in the back of her head. She let Triple G take control of the thrusting. She held her position over top of Triple G and allowed him to hammer up into her gushiness. The more her lover pumped into her, the more she squirted her butter on his loaf of bread. Mimi was stupid wet; Triple could feel her juices trickle down his nut sack and down through the crack of his ass.

Milky cum residue started formulating at the base of Triple G's rod, and the sight provoked him to hammer away into Mimi until he shot his load in Mimi like a 44 mag—one big squirt—and coated her walls. Triple G pulled Mimi to him where she collapsed on his chest. They both laid still until their heartbeats found the same rhythm. "Triple, I got to pee, baby!" Mimi announced, coming off Triple G's limp penis. She headed to the bathroom to relieve herself and wash her amazing coochie. Triple didn't say anything; he just watched Mimi's sexy tattooed body sway from side to side as she disappeared into the bathroom.

Triple G grabbed the pre-roll blunt that was resting in the ashtray next to the bed on the nightstand. He struck a match and lit the grade 4 weed. He took a few pulls from the exotic before retrieving his phone and checked it for any missed calls or texts. He had none. He dialed Spook's number. The phone rang four times before it went to voicemail; this had been the norm since the attempt on his life. And this shit really had him nervous. Triple G had been calling Spook, but the nigga Spook hadn't answered his phone or returned any of Triple G's texts. He had Mimi text and call from her phone but it was the same result.

Triple G still didn't feel that Spook had sent them wolves to claim this life. He was feeling like the hit came directly from the Cartel. There was no way that Spook would honor a hit on him. Triple and Mimi wanted to believe that, but his heart was saying something totally different. He dialed the number again and was once again met with Spook's voicemail again. He let out a large cloud of smoke and logged on to his social media platforms. He was hoping that Spook was locked up and if that was the case it would be all over social media because Spook wasn't the type of nigga that goes to jail quietly; his status alone wouldn't allow it. There was not on social media any news about Spook. For some reason Triple G went to Spook's profile picture. Triple G noticed that Spook's profile picture had been changed; this gave Triple G that answer he was looking for. This confirmed that Spook was alive and well. When Triple G saw what Spook's profile picture had been changed, the weed he was smoking on got caught in this throat and sent him into a coughing fit. He knew shit had just got all the way the fuck real. Triple jumped out of bed and started packing his shit.

Jibril Williams

Chapter Seven

Billie walked in the DC Superior Courtroom. She wanted to draw less attention to herself as possible, but that was a hard task to accomplish when you was a white woman built like Nicki Minaj. Even though she wore a plain black jean, a Dior V-neck T-shirt, she still couldn't help but draw attention to herself. All eyes fell on her and her sexy looks. Paranoia had no siege her mind, and she was fighting desperately to maintain her composure. Her eyes darted back and forth behind her dark Prada shades; she felt that the Marshall would swap down on her at any minutes. She pushed them thoughts to the back of her head and found an empty seat next to the aisle. She had the chance to meet up with two of the best lawyers that the District of Columbia had to offer. She gave both lawyers thirty thousand apiece, and she was pleased to see both lawyers sitting at the front of the courtroom waiting on their respectable clients to be brought out. The courtroom was packed with news reporters and spectators trying to get the scoop and glimpse of The Cop Killer and Genital Killer man that was tied to the notorious Red Bottom jewelry store robbers.

The attorneys already informed Billie that all they were here to do today was to find out what Phatmama and Racks were being charged with and see if they could get a bond hearing. There was a man standing in front of the judge. The man was just led in by a group of Marshalls. Billie only got a side glimpse of him, but she strangely found him attractive. The courts stated his name: *MacArthur Williams* v. District of Columbia. He was being charged for one count of first-degree murder for killing a government witness. Billie sat staring at his back. For some strange reason she wanted to know him better. But she remembered Sticks, then that notion quickly vanished from her mind. MacArthur was quickly escorted out the courtroom just as briefly he was brought in it. He was denied bail, and a bail hearing was scheduled for a later date in front of another judge. Billie hope that he would make bail at his next hearing, but she knew that was wishful thinking because the chances of the District of Columbia granting bail to someone on murder charges were slim; Billie knew this because she googled the statistics before she met up with the lawyers.

Her thoughts turned to Tata, and the thought of Tata thinking about killing her had her feeling uneasy. If the friendship between her and Phatmama wasn't as strong as it was, she would have murdered Tata as soon as she laid the FN down. She couldn't really blame Tata for being leery of her due to the current circumstances. It still bothered her because she hasn't done nothing but shown Tata and the Red Bottom Squad her undeniable loyalty.

Seeing Racks and Phatmama being brought out the back of the courtroom broke Billie's thoughts immediately. She became hot and she felt sweat starting to trickle down her armpits. The courtroom AC didn't do any justice to hinder the moistness formulating under her arms. Billie placed her hand over her chest and the beating of her heart could be felt easily. Racks looked broken and frail. Racks was moving slow with a female Marshall walking closely behind her. Billie knew Racks was still recovering from the assault Jelli and her goons had placed on her. But Billie wondered if Racks looking the way she did was due to the police jumping on her for killing a police officer. Billie's face bunched up seeing Phatmama in her paper jumper. You could damn near see through the fabric. If it wasn't for Phatmama wearing panties and bra under the paper jumper, you would be able to see her goodies. But Phatmama still had her head held high. She wasn't gonna let them break her state of mind. The court clerk called out Phatmama and Racks' name and the proceeding began.

"Tanya Foxx and Rochelle Banks v. District of Columbia."

The court clerk handed the judge two files. Hearing their clients' name, Danny Onoranto and Dale Allen rushed through the partition that separated the court from the spectators. Danny Onoranto stood next to Phatmama, and Dale Allen stood next to Banks. Both lawyers handed their clients their cards.

"Your honor, Danny Onoranto here representing Ms. Foxx in this matter," Onoranto stated firmly in his deep voice.

"Dale Allen here representing Ms. Banks," the short puggy lawyer stated, adjusting his designer glasses on this face.

"Well, I see that Ms. Foxx well as Ms. Banks have hired the big guns. I would take pleasure to see how you two prize fighting attorneys will be pre-format trial!" Judge Penny Wagner said from the bench. She had heard many amazing things about both lawyers on how they perform at trial and how they both had the ability to win the minds and hearts of any jury. Both lawyers smiled humbly at Judge Wagner. They knew this was an arraignment proceeding and there was no need to charm the judge with words.

"Your honor, the government request that both defendants be kept in custody," the prosecutor said, flipping through some papers, before he contrived. "These two individuals belong to the all-female gang that has been terrorizing the District of Columbia, by robbing jewelry stores as well as a bank.

"Your honor, as of this time, there's no proof that my client is who the government say she is or did any of the things the government is accusing her of. We request that she be released on her own personal recognizance!" Mr. Onoranto stated while straightening his tie.

"I'm in agreeance with Mr. Onoranto. There's nothing on my client also to keep her held in custody," Mr. Allen capped.

Phatmama was intensely listening to her lawyer speak on her behalf. She was surprised that she even had a lawyer there representing instead of one of the overworked public defender lawyers that the court appoints when you don't have the funds and the means to have a paid attorney on speed dial. Phatmama never heard of the lawyer's name before but she could tell by the way the judge had greeted him he was someone she respected. Phatmama flipped the card over that she held in her hand. Red ink scribbled on the back of the attorney card caught her attention: "Red Bottoms stand tall", and a number she never seen stared back at her. Phatmama turned her head slightly to the left and started scanning the courtroom. She smiled when she saw Billie sitting among the spectators looking sexy in a pair of dark shades. She nodded in acknowledgement and Billie nodded back. Phatmama turned on her back and faced the judge.

"Your honor, Ms. Foxx and Ms. Banks are very dangerous. Ms. Foxx is not only being charged with a string of robberies, but she has been fingered in the high-profile cases that have plagued the district of Columbia for months now. It has been declared that Ms. Foxx is no other than the District of Columbia Genital Killer. Also, Ms. Banks will be charged with the murder of metropolitan police officer. Ms. Banks was fingered as the shooter of Officer Spencer whom she murdered."

Judge Wagner looked over her round-rim glasses at Phatmama and Racks before administrating her ruling. She wondered what was transpiring in the two women's lives to have encouraged them to participate in such crime of violence. "Personal recognizance is denied. Remand both defendants to Central Treatment Facility. Mr. Onoranto, Mr. Dale, you can request for a bail hearing in front of the trial judge."

Both lawyers knew it was highly and unlikely that the women would be granted a bond, but they knew with all the charges their client was being charged with—They knew it was going to take more than a skillful mouth to get them off. The women were going to need God himself to help them overcome what they were facing. The judge called the next case, and the Marshall escorted Racks and Phatmama in the courtroom.

Jibril Williams

Chapter Eight

Fate brushed a pecan brown complexioned hand over his salt-and-peppered beard. He nursed a glass of Dusse in his right hand. He was in deep thought as a chess player would be, thinking about his next best move. There was no doubt that his next move needed to be his best move, or it would be his last move. He knocked back the shot of Dusse with ease and allowed the warm liquid to slither down his throat and burn his empty stomach. The tension in his neck was tight; he could feel the muscle in his neck knot up. He refilled his glass and reflected more on his current situation. The connect wanted to meet with him asap. The last time that he had met Weedy face to face, Weedy had made it clear that whatever happened to Jelli best needed to happen to him. He already knew meeting with Weedy would likely lead to an early grave. What could he do? Flee? That would be very uncharacteristic of him. Weedy had already threatened to bring harm to his family if Jelli wasn't protected and kept out of harm way. How the hell he was to keep her out of harm's way when she feeling herself! Killing muthafuckers in a room full of niggas, flaunting around the crib with a crown of a dead woman on her head. Jelli crossed the line when she killed Diego in front of him. Diego was Cain's nephew. The nephew of a man she claimed to love and whom she professed was the centerpiece of her life. If Cain meant so much to her how could she kill his nephew like a stray dog. Fate helped his boss Cain raise Diego. What was he to do? Just let Jelli kill Diego without no repercussions? Fate closed his eyes and exhaled; he could still smell the stench of gunpowder from Jelli's gun discharging.

   Every time he smelled the unique odor, his mind immediately turned back to Diego. It hurt him more when he had the task of dumping Diego's body. Leaving the kid in that alley like he was trash had him fucked all the way up.

Fate acted on impulse and did the unthinkable. After he found out Jelli was locked up on a gun charge, he informed the police that the gun Jelli was arrested with was indeed the murder weapon of the man's body that was found in Newton Street alley. Jelli was charged with Diego's murder after ballistics was performed on the gun Jelli was caught with and the bullet that was removed from Diego's head was determined to be a match.

Fate wasn't going to testify against Jelli. He knew a murder charge would have Jelli sitting over CTF for at least eighteen to twenty-four months fighting the charges. By that time Fate would be able to take the wheel of Cain Crime family and run as his own. Fate knew the move was a bitch move but as long as his secret can stay in the dark, he could live with it. Once Jelli's charges were dismissed, he will deal her the same fate she gave Diego and place a bullet to the back of the head. Right now Weedy posed the greater threat at the moment. Fate had a move up his sleeve and he hoped that he could pull it off and if not, he would be joining Cain and Diego soon. Fate knocked the second shot of Dusse. He sat the glass down on the table in front of him and picked up the picture that sat next to the fifth of Dusses.

Jelli was on her fifth set of squats. She once read that your legs were like tree roots. If the roots of a tree were weak then the tree would be easy to push over. Jelli saw the legs were roots to her freedom so she kept them strong and light. If her legs were strong, it would hard for someone to knock her down during a fight. The more she squatted, the more she thought about the bitches who stole her shit and how their broke petty ass action caused her to act out and get locked in the hole. She wished she could have gotten all of them that were involved.

She stopped her count at twenty-five and walked to the back of her cell, and did twenty-five jumping-jacks. Her thoughts next went to Fate. She put it in her mind that Fate would be the next person she would kill once she got out. She wasn't feeling his disappearing, and her intuition was telling her him feeding ghosting her was done intentionally. She had an entire empire out there that she couldn't help it growing because she was in jail; this thought alone frustrated her. She went and took a seat on the toilet to work through her thoughts. Her mind was running too rapidly for her to think standing on her feet. Then it hit her; it all came together so vividly. Fate falling back from her was because he was now in the position to take control of Cain Crime Family since she was locked in jail. He had all the means to take control. He had the plug and he already had control over the men to keep the operation moving forward. Jelli felt like a fucking dummie. How could she ever think Fate could be loyal to her!

Fate was Cain's right-hand man, not hers. But the thought of Fate leaving her in this position without assistance made her wish she would have shot him when she killed Diego. The tap on her cell door got her attention.

"Roberts, you have a legal. Get dressed!" C.O. James said, peering through the door at Jelli.

"Okay, give me about ten minutes and I'll be ready." Jelli started grabbing her toothbrush and tube of Bob Barker toothpaste at her foot locker. This was all she had until she was able to make it to commissary. She just hoped she should make it before she saw the adjustment board and they sanction her beating Meek's ass.

Jelli brushed her teeth and washed her face quickly. She sat bare ass on the stainless steel toilet bare skin without lining the toilet with toilet paper before she sat down. Hole time was hard; you didn't have the privilege of having extra toilet paper to place a barrier between your ass cheeks and the toilet. After emptying her bladder and washing her hands, she called at the crack of her door to C.O. James that she was ready for her legal visit.

When Jelli made it inside the legal visiting room, her attorney—Ms. McNeal—was waiting on her. The lawyer was reviewing some documents when Jelli walked in. Jelli rolled her eyes at her attorney. Ms. James removed the handcuffs from Jelli's wrist. "Notify the officer in the booth when you are done," C.O. James informed Ms. McNeal before she left the room. Ms. McNeal looked up from the documents and nodded in agreement.

"Hello, Ms. Roberts!" Ms. McNeal greeted Jelli in a warble tone. Jelli looked at her with her face scrunched up like Ms. McNeal's breath smelt like bad pussy. Jelli been sitting over in the dirty ass jail almost eighteen days now and this is the second time she had seen Ms. McNeal. Jelly had been blowing the lawyer's phone every chance she got just like she was calling Fate. Ms. McNeal wasn't available due to her having to represent another client at trial. Well, that was the spill Ms. McNeal's secretary would convey to Jelli when she called.

"Ms. McNeal, I don't know who the fuck you may think I am but I'm the wrong bitch to play games with." Jelli's words were loaded with malice. "I done had you paid top dollars for you to represent me. So from now on when I call for you then it should be in your best interest to come and see me."

Ms. McNeal was a warrior in D.C Superior courtroom. Her pale face turned flush red with embarrassment and anger.

Jelli was verbally abusing her. She might have been a concession woman but she was bred from them gritty streets of DC, and them same streets taught not to take no shit from no one.

"Excuse me, check your tone first and foremost—and secondly, you have to be open-minded enough to know that you are not the only client I have on retainer. I prioritize my time between my clients based on their court date and court status. You just hired me as your attorney, but there are others before you. If you cannot respect that fact and respect me as your attorney, then you have a decision to make. You can hire another attorney or hire another one that's willing to kiss your ass. I have no problem returning your money, minus the cause to me to make a court appearance and for me to sit with you doing your little meeting with the D.A." Ms. McNeal spoke to Jelli with attitude and authority.

Jelli locked eyes with the semi-attractive lawyer. She was contemplating the idea of having another lawyer step in, but Jelli knew it would only slow her process down. Jelli let out a sigh.

"What's the status of them letting me outta here?" Jelli said sadly. Ms. McNeal let her own sigh out before she addressed
Jelli's question. "We have a lot to accomplish before that can happen."

"What you mean? I gave them the Red Bottom Squad? I told them everything I knew about the robbery and the murders at the cemetery. The bank robbery and the murders. I even told about them killing Rico. Why am I still seating in jail? They said they would grant me immunity and I can walk on the murder charge for killing Diego." Jelli pleaded. Ms. McNeal looked at her client like she was crazy. Ms. McNeal took a deep breath before she pushed the documents to the side she was reading when Jelli was brought in the room. She placed her hands on the wooden table that was bolted to the floor. It was clear to her that Jelli didn't have a clue to what she have gotten herself into.

When Jelli was caught with the gun that killed Diego, she was so quick to make a deal to get out of jail but she was there today to break some bad news to Jelli.

"Ms. Roberts, things are not as easy as you have thought they were. Everyone wants their pound of flesh. The District of Columbia did grant you immunity, but you are on Federal probation and the Feds still can charge you with that gun you was arrested with. The Feds wants their pound of flesh. They didn't grant you immunity. Once DC is done with you on the Superior Court level, the Feds will be to see you. The Feds have placed a hold on you for the gun. Your probation has been violated. The District of Columbia want the Red Bottom Squad. But the Feds want an individual." Ms. McNeal shuffled through some papers. "Do you happen to know a man by the name of Weedy? They want your Canadian connect."

Chapter Ten

"Ruffle your fingers through your hair. Come on, don't be shy!" The C.O. screamed and barked orders at the new arrivals at CTF— Correctional Treatment Facility. A group of women stood naked in front the bad body C.O. The woman reminded Phatmama of Big Freeda. "Lift them titties up," Big Freeda said as she walked the line of women, inspecting titties for contraband. Racks mugged the C.O. viciously. Being naked in front of a group of people was doing something to her mental. She was ready to snap.

"Okay, everyone, turn around backs towards me. Bend over at the waist. I want to see that brown eye. Not the one you wink out of, but the one you fart, poop and stink out of." A few of the women laughed and giggled at the C.O.'s sarcastic remark. "Don't stand back up until I tap you in the back." Racks never complied with the C.O.'s orders. This was the most demoralizing treatment that goes on when you are being processed into any jail or prison. Racks had a problem with this. She could never get comfortable with busting her ass open for no one. She knew that it was gonna take place regardless, but she wasn't going do it with a smile. "Hey, Ms. Attitude. What? You don't speak English or something? I said bend the fuck over and spread your fuck ass!" Big Freeda said aggressively.

Racks turned and faced the woman. Murder rolled her eyes, and Big Freeda felt the cold chill of them. "What type of bitch you is looking up muthafuckas' asses?" Racks spluttered through clenched teeth. Racks balled her fist up. She wasn't in no condition to fight but she was ready to bump with Big Freeda about showing her ass.

"Bitch, if you don't turn your dyke ass."

"Hold up, listen!" Phatmama said, turning around to face Big Freeda. Phatmama had to do something because she was not about to let Big Freeda jump on Racks. They would be in a no-win situation. Big Freeda would call for back up and it would put her and Racks to be fighting toe to toe with about fifty C.O.'s. "Have you heard about the Red Bottom Squad?" The C.O. balled her face up as if she was about to say something slick. But she immediately fixed her face. She had been keeping up with all the robberies the all-female crew was pulling off. She low key admired the ladies. Big Freeda's facial expression validated that she did know about the Red Bottom Squad. "You in the presence of the Red Bottom Squad and from the news you know that we are about two things—that muthafucking bag and that muthafucking life. You embrace and respect us, we show love but you bring harm then know we come wearing red bottoms and busting fully loaded weapons. So what it's gonna be?" Phatmama spoke loud enough for Big Freeda to hear her. Phatmama peeped the C.O.'s name tag and it read: *Flowers*.

C.O. Flowers was taken aback by how Phatmama and Racks showed no fear. She didn't know how to respond. She did what was best for her. "I'm for the empowerment of women."

"Good," Phatmama said. "Give her a pass on the sucka shit and I promise you your good deed won't go unforgotten."

C.O. Flowers nodded in agreement. The incident had her slightly shook. She continued down the row of women, tapping them on their backs so they could stand up right.

After leaving R & D (Receive and Discharge), Phatmama and Racks were escorted to the infirmary, where they gave up urine samples and blood samples. They were as also tested for TB, HIV and to see if they were pregnant. While Phatmama was waiting for Racks to come out from seeing the lab tech who would administrate the HIV testing, a Unity care worker approached Phatmama and asked her how do it feel to chop a man's ding-a-ling off. She was thinking about chopping off her boyfriend dick because he had been cheating on her and gave her a transmitted disease. Phatmama couldn't believe that the woman just admitted that to her.

The media coverage had CTF buzzing about Phatmama and Racks. Phatmama was tired of it already. She wanted to get in the cell to process her thoughts and try to find some sleep. She already knew calling Billie would have to wait until tomorrow, due to it being so late. The C.O. escorted her and Racks for Medical and stopped at housing *Unit A*.

***

Kirby sat back in a chair inside the unit control bubble, flipping through car magazine. The Porsche Taycan was pure beauty. The four-hundred-and-something horsepower was a different type of beast on the road. Kirby could see himself riding clean in an all-red one, pulling up on all the hoes. Kirby looked at his Casio: it was 9:30 and he had about two hours before he clocked off work.

"Unit A, escort at your gate!" Kirby's radio squeaked. Kirby took his feet off the side of the control panel and placed them back on the floor. He stood and looked through the bubble. He popped the grill off and let the escort in. Ms. Lowe came in accompanied with two arrivals. Kirby exited the bubble with his clip board in hand.

"What we got, Ms. Lowe?" Kirby asked, not even paying attention to the two women in their presence. "We got Ms. Fox and Ms. Banks. These are the women that the news have been going crazy about."

Kirby's eyes fell on Phatmama and Racks. He had seen the two recently somewhere. His eyes locked in Racks DCB tattoo that held a spot on the right side of her neck.

"Oh, Ms. Lowe, I got them from here," Kirby said. Ms. Gene popped the gate, and Ms. Lowe left, leaving Kirby and the females alone in the sally port. Kirby peeped over his shoulder to find Ms. Gene on the phone.

"You DCB?" Kirby asked, looking at Racks.

"That's my bloodline."

"Sticks is my cousin. You know him?"

"Sticks is the big homie. He's as blood as they come," Racks said.

"I'm gonna call Sticks tonight. Anything you want me to tell him?"

"Yeah, tell him that Racks and Phatmama is over CTF and I need a small phone. And let him know to let Whip know I need money on the books asap."

"I'm on it soon as I get off work," Kirby said with excitement in his voice. "Right now I have to assign you all a cell. Do you want a cell together?" Kirby asked.

"Yeah," Phatmama and Rack said in chorus.

"Alright, come on. You both going to cell twelve. The two that live in the cell before you had a fight. The chick Roberts beat her celly bad with a few bars of soap tied in a sock." Phatmama didn't like dude; he talked too much. She could tell he was lame as fuck. The unit was already locked in for the night.

"When is rec time for tomorrow?"

"8:30 a.m. Breakfast is at 6:30," Kirby said, stopping in front of cell twelve. Ms. Gene was watching him because soon as he stopped in front of the cell, the cell door slid open. Racks and Phatmama stepped in and the door closed behind them. "Racks, hold your head. I come on at two p.m.," Kirby said, walking away.

Kirby was smiling hard as fuck on the inside. He couldn't wear the smile on his face because he knew every muthafucka was at their door watching the new arrivals that he just brought in. He went straight to the bathroom to call Sticks. He'd been waiting on the opportunity to get down with DCB gang; he may just find his chance.

Jibril Williams

Chapter Eleven

"Flame my nigga, I hope everything is on the up and up about this shit," Whip said, leaning up from the back of the stolen car. He clutched a black fo' fifth. This gun was grabbed by a black leathered gloved hand. He stared at Flame with blood-shot eyes. Flame sat in the front passenger seat with a sawed-off Mossberg shotgun on this lap. Before he could respond to Whip, Sticks' phone vibrated.

"Yeah, who this?" Stick answered the phone. Sticks didn't say much; he just listened. "They fam, Kirby, swing past the club tonight so we can put some things in play," Sticks spoke into the phone. His eyes met Whip's in the rear mirror before he hung up the phone. Sticks didn't bring to the light who was on the phone. Whip took it as though he didn't want to talk in front of Flame.

"Whip, the lick is what it is. I put it on my B's!" Flame stated calmly, still watching their potential target. "I been sticking the nigga hard as fuck before he got let that bitch murder him."

Whip's heart rate went up a few beats hearing this nigga address Phatmama as *bitch*; he didn't know Phatmama was the shadow behind the gun in Cain's death and he had every intention to leave it that way. He was sensitive about Flame's choice of words because Phatmama was his nigga Boot's lady. And to have disrespect Phatmama in his presence was to disrespect Boot. And he wouldn't let it go the next time.

"I know the ins and outs of his operation." Flame pulled his hat down farther over his eyes. Sticks sat behind the wheel of the stolen Buick. He adjusted the Mack 11 that was resting on his lap. He blew O's in the air from the Newport 100 he puffed on. His thoughts were on business and the task at hand. Flame used to work for Cain. His boss took a liking to him and embraced him and placed him in a position to be distributor in Oxon Hill, Maryland. He had his own set of Bloods that he network Cain's product through. They called themselves *The Flame Boys*. Flame was smart and he was always looking for a better opportunity to advance to the next level in the drug trade. And that fact alone had him sitting in a stolen car holding a twelve-gauge sawed-off.

Flame came to Whip with a power move. He would disclose intimate details about Cain Crime Family operation. Whip will invade the traps and the money houses. Once Fate and Jelli are out the way, Whip will become his plug and he would take control of Cain Crime Family distributors. Whip and Sticks didn't fully trust his show of faith with them on this move tonight. A blue Caddie STS turned the corner on the block of P Street SE. The Caddie drove through the block like any other car would, but a few minutes later the Caddie emerged back on the block and parked in front of the white house where Whip and them sat across from.

"That's the lick right there," Flame said, sliding down in his seat. Whip and Sticks followed. They could hear the Caddie open and close. A tall light-skinned chick got out wearing a gray, pinstripe business suit. She looked very professional, standing on four-inch heels. But she seemed out of place based on her attire and being on P Street. She walked to the back of the Caddie while she had her phone glued to her ear. "Girl, I don't have time for this little boy ass—yeah, he have a big ole dick but I need more than that, and sitting home calling all day playing games isn't working for me!" the light-skinned chick said into her phone. She opened the trunk and removed a book bag. Her eyes fell on the Buick and they paused there for about thirty seconds.

"Girl, I'm about to handle this business for Fate then I'm going to head your way. The Dusse is on you. Bye, bitch!" the light-skinned chick said, disconnecting.

A hand wrapped around her mouth and she felt pressure in the back of her head, then her lights went out. She would never get a chance to meet up with her girl for the scheduled drink. Whip's fo' fifth flashed in his hand. The silencer he had attached to the gun killed the loud boom the gun normally would have made. Whip threw her limp body in the back of the open STS trunk and closed it. The chick was so engrossed in her phone call she didn't hear or see Whip creep from the Buick and double around the car on her. Whip sat the book bag on the trunk of the car and checked it. He was pleased to see it was stuffed with five bricks. He closed the book bag and pushed his arms through the straps and stationed the bag on his back. He gave the thumbs up to Flame and Sticks who were sitting in the Buick. Everything went in fast motion. They both exited the car, running towards the white house. Sticks threw two canisters through the house windows. One was a flashbang and the other was tear gas. Both canisters discharged with a loud bang. Flame slipped his gas mask over his face and gave the door a firm kick; the door flew off the frame. He was the first one in the house. Sticks and Whip came in behind him wearing gas masks and packing heat. Two niggas were at the living room table counting money and the other was on the couch playing games on the Xbox. The flashbang and the tear gas had them on the floor fighting to breathe and gather their equilibrium. Flame's shotgun blast shredded one of the dude's upper body from the buck shots that it released. Sticks tapped the trigger on the Mack, and a short burst of bullets sprang from the deadly weapon, finding marks into Fate's workers, killing them instantly with head and chest shots.

They moved quickly, placing the money that was on the table into trash bags that was lying next to the table. Flame knew that there was always four people in the house at all times; there was no need to check the rest of the house. Whip sent the fo'fifth spitting in his hand, putting two holes in his target's head. Flame's victim struggled to breathe; the buck shots had his chest open, but he was still alive. Whip tapped his trigger once, giving ole boy a good night slug to the dome. "Let's move!" Whip announced, leading the way out the house, leaving behind nothing but murder and mayhem. The murders he committed tonight hadn't in the least eased the pain of losing Boot, but there were so many more lives to take before he could ever heal from this.

Chapter Twelve

Kirby pulled up at Club Red Bottomz. The club didn't seem to be stagnated by the raid. He couldn't believe the sexy owner, Tata, was wanted for a string of sophisticated robberies and murder. Kirby had seen her face plastered all over the news. He figured that bad bitches go as hard as niggas for that bag. Outside, the club's parking lot was packed with all type of cars that were way out of his price range. He would have to pull over time at CTF for a whole year before he would be able to purchase one of the luxury automobile that was decorating the parking lot. Kirby saw a triple red Maybach S600 sitting so sexy in the parking lot. He wanted to get out his Ford Focus and prostrate to the foreign whip because that muthafucka was a work of God.

Naw, the search for the club owner definitely haven't slowed the club action down, Kirby thought to himself. He figured that muthafuckas wanted to see some ass and titties no matter what the owner's personal issues were. Kirby parked his car and walked through the club's mahogany doors. After paying his admission, he was permitted into the club. He was greeted by the loud music. *Throat Baby* was playing through the club's speakers.

Kirby found the red and black interior dope as fuck. Inside the club was laced with thick beautiful women. He smiled and licked his chapped lips at a dancer that walked past him, giving him that *come-and-play-in-my-throat* look. The white lace boy shorts was being eaten alive with every step she took. The pair of Red Bottoms she had on had her legs looking fit and toned. She was bare chested and held a fist full of bills. You could tell she was busting the club down. Kirby adjusted his dick through his jeans. He could only imagine what the stripper could do on a pole and his dick. He hit the bar and ordered a double shot of Henny and sent Sticks a quick text, letting him know he was in the club. Kirby was checking out the bartender; she was thicker than a snicker. The name on her shirt read: Cindy. She smiled at him. She could tell that he was overwhelmed by her beauty and her perky breasts. But she could tell he was broke by the clothes he wore and the lack of drip that wasn't present. She could also tell that he wanted to say something to her but didn't know what to use as an icebreaker; most men were intimidated by her looks, and that was a turn-off to her. The dude who kept eye-balling her lacked confidence to step up to the plate, but once he had a few shots of double Henny, his confidence would be on one thousand and she wanted to be long gone by the time that happened. Kirby downed the double shot and ordered another one.

"Aye, babygirl!" the chick who just walked up to the door next to Kirby yelled, trying to get the attention of the bartender who just made her way to the end of the bar to service another customer. The woman next to Kirby was a work of greatness. The tattoos enhanced and highlighted her beauty. The flaming red hair blended skillfully in her light-skinned complexion. The bartender came to retrieve the money the five-two snack was waving.

"Can I get you something, baby?" Cindy asked, sexually eying the customer. She could tell she wasn't a DC native.

"Yeah, send five bottles of Dusse and five bottes of Moet and five bottles Aquafina water over to that table and—" The woman stopped talking in mid-sentence because she felt Kirby eyes burning a hole in the side of her face. He was about to say something to the beautiful lady that was ordering all the bottles. But the stare she gave him was so cold it made his words get lost in his throat. She could smell a lame a mile away, and the nigga beside her was nothing more and nothing less. She turned her attention back to the bartender who burst out laughing about the red-headed boss checking her without words.

"Like a bitch said before we were interrupted, send the bottles over to that table and send over tonight top five dancers, and make them thick."

"You don't have to worry about the women—they definitely
come thick, that's what Red Bottomz specialize in. We only have thick entertainments."

"Okay, we'll see," the lady said and walked away. Kirby peeped over his shoulder and caught a glimpse of the red bone's backside; he was impressed. His phone vibrated on the bar top. It was a text from Sticks, telling him to come to the office. Sticks gave him instruction on how to locate the office. He downed his drink and made a beeline to the club office.

Before he could knock on the office door, it was open and he was met by Sticks and a cloud of smoke that instantly gave him a contact. He hoped bro didn't have to take a urine for his job no time soon.

"What's up, blood?" Sticks greeted his cousin with a pound.
"Slow motion, my nigga, trying to get in where I fit in!" Kirby capped. When he got in the office, he caught Whip placing a square package in the desk drawers he was sitting behind. A pile of money was resting on the desk. Kirby nodded at Whip, acknowledging his presence. He remembered the last time he saw Whip. Whip wasn't too kind to his presence. So he didn't have too much to say to him. Whip didn't nod back in acknowledgement.

"We was kinda in the middle of something, fam, so let's get to it. What's good, Kirby?" Sticks stated, leaning against the office door after he closed it and secured the locks.

Kirby stuck his hands in his pockets and took a deep breath before he started talking. He was hoping he could capitalize off the info he was about to convey to Whip and his cousin—Sticks.

"Tonight while I was at work two broads came into the unit I'm assigned to." Whip sat back in his chair and listened half-heartedly. "One of them had a DCB tattoo on her neck. She said her name was Racks. She was with a thick-boned chick named Phatmama." Hearing Racks and Phatmama's name, Whip sat up in his chair. Kirby had his full attention. "The broad—Racks—told me to tell she needs some paper on her account and that she needs a phone," Kirby said, pointing at Sticks. "I wrote down both of their government names and other deets." Kirby handed a piece of paper to Sticks. Whip pushed his bifocals back on the bridge of his nose. Sticks had conveyed to him that they could use Kirby. Whip really didn't think so, but he was glad that he gave Kirby them three bands the night they met at Red Bottomz' grand opening. He was happy that Sticks' words came into full intuition. Whip reached his hand out for the piece of paper Sticks held with Racks and Phatmama's name on it. Whip leaned back in his chair and plucked the piece of paper he held. He stared at Kirby. Kirby couldn't read Whip's eyes through the thick lenses of his glasses; the lenses of Whip's glasses were thick like ice cubes.

"Sticks' been telling me that you want to become a full active member of DCB. Is this true?" Whip asked. This was his first time directly addressing Kirby.

Kirby been waiting a long time to be officially branded as a blood, especially a DCB. He couldn't believe it was not gonna happen right here in club Red Bottomz. "Yeah, that's what it is, Blood," Kirby stumbled with his words.

Whip got to his feet and walked slowly around the desk. Kirby thought he was gonna give him that face-to-face stare down. But Whip walked right past him and stopped in front of the hundred-gallon fish tank that was located against the wall. Inside the tank was a school of red belly piranhas. The ten fish swam together as one. The piranhas were the size of a *Ms. Freshley's* oatmeal pie. The fish looked deadly, and their sharp teeth that set on display were there to do damage at a moment's notice. Whip waved Kirby over to where he stood. "You see them?" Whip asked. Kirby for the first time noticed that the fish were piranhas. He nodded to Whip's question. "These Piranhas represent our family—DCB. We are the vicious, dangerous and relentless. We move on one accordance. That's what make DCB a force not to be fucked with. Do you know what happen, my nigga, when muthafuckas step out of line and disrupt our flow, disrupt our unison?"

Kirby swallowed hard; he mustered the word "No" out his mouth. He looked over to Sticks, who gave him a look that said he's in a grown man arena.

"Well, since you don't know, then let me show you," Whip said, turning the light on to another tank that was located below the hundred-gallon tank. About ten white mice scrambled around the tank when Whip hit the tank light. Whip stuck his hand in the ten gallon tank and snatched a mouse up by the tail. He opened the lid of the Piranha tank. The fish looked wicked floating over black gravel and black crystals that rested at the bottom of the tank. Whip dropped the mice in the water, and the deadly fish attacked their prey relentlessly. The fish ate the mouse alive by biting small chunks out its small body. The assault on the mouse created a craze in the water. Blood and small pieces of rodent polluted the tank's water. The piranhas swam through the water, plucking the remains of the mouse until there was nothing left for them to feast on.

"There's a certain beast that must live in you to be labeled as a DCB," Whip stated, sizing Kirby up." You got to have that heart of a savage in you. Do you think you have what it takes to be in this family?" Whip asked.

Kirby nodded. All he ever wanted was to be officially put on by an official blood set. He could have joined any blood set, but he felt none was official except DCB because he had seen how they networked, and his cousin was affiliated to the gang.

Whip stared into Kirby's eyes. He saw that he had some drive and determination in his eyes. But Whip didn't know if he had the heart to be placed in the ranks of DCB. But he was gonna try and see how Kirby plans out. "First thing first, we giving you a name change. That Kirby shit is lame as fuck. From now on your handle is *Super K*."

Kirby smiled, hearing the new name selected for him. He was ready to put some work in for family. But Whip had other plans. Whip walked over to the desk and scooped up a stack of bills and tossed them to Kirby. "Handle that business with Phatmama and Racks."

Kirby caught the money that was bundled by a red rubber band in the air. "Say less," he mumbled.

"Don't fuck this up, Super K, as of right now this is your only job in this family. Make sure that Racks and Phatmama is straight at all time while being housed at CTF. If things go smoothly then we advance you to the next level and if you pass that, then and only then you will have a seat at this table."

Whip studied Super K's body language. "This shit already done. They both will be calling you tomorrow letting you know I handle business," Super K replied. A knock came to the door, interrupting the meeting. Kirby stuffed the money in his pocket and Whip went to open the door. He was taken aback when he found Triple G standing on the other side of the door with a bottle of Dusse in his hand.

"Suu Wuu," Triple G said, throwing his hands in the air.

Jibril Williams

Chapter Thirteen

Phatmama washed the dirty wash cloth out and hung it on the side of the sink to dry. She took a seat on the stainless steel toilet and watched Racks sleep. The girl was mumbling and talking in her sleep. A few times she had heard Racks whisper Zoey's name and immediately made Phatmama think about her slain friend. She smiled to herself, remembering how Zoey was always trained to go. She was always down to get her hands bloody for her team. Phatmama smiled harder, thinking about how Zoey had a crazy addiction for Blow Pops. She kept a different kind of sucker in her mouth. She missed Zoey clearly.

Phatmama was tired as hell, but her body wouldn't allow her to shut down. She had way too much going on in her head and heart to allow herself any type of rest. When Phatmama and Racks got into their cell, she told Racks to lay down and she cleaned the cell with a bar of soap and wash cloth that was issued to her when she was processed through R & D. She was just through washing herself up.

She inhaled and exhaled deeply, closing her eyes. Her nightmare was rebirthed. Vision of Boot's body twitching and jerking from the barrage of a bullets the police shot into him. All day she was fighting not to think about the raid that claimed her lover's life. But she was alone and trapped to deal with her thoughts and demons. The midnight shift C.O.'s had already come through and counted them. Flashes of Boot being hit with so many bullets lived so vividly in her mind. She could still smell the gunpowder in the air and feel the slick feeling of Boot's blood on her hands. Repeatedly, she could see the police Glocks spark over and over in slow motion like a motion picture. With every spark she could see Boot's body being hit with a copper bullet. She knew she would never be able to touch her lover again; their hearts would never have the privilege to beat as one again. Her tears fell freely as the summer rain. Boot was forever gone. Her knight, her ruler, her sadistic heart was gone. More tears fell free from her eyes. Phatmama felt like a hole was sitting in the middle of her chest. The pain she felt was intolerable. She wished it was her that had died; she wished she would have died right along with Boot. The police came to the house to arrest her. How in the fuck the situation ended in Boot's death and her going to jail!

Phatmama squeezed eyes tight, trying her best to slow the fall of her tears. She balled her fist in frustration. She was mad at God for allowing Boot to be a casualty. How could she be born so innocent and pure but plagued with so much hardship and pain in her short life. Being a black woman in America, being abused as a child, being in the military and raped by those she gave an oath to protect. The loss of Boot. *Fuck God! He is the real savage because I never did anything to him for me to be punished the way I have been. How could life be so damn malevolent, so wicked*! Phatmama had heard of stories of people losing a lover. She never imagined the pain they experienced; now she was living it. She was feeling its rawest pain. She wondered whether Jelli felt this exact pain; she wondered if this was Karma for taking Cain away from Jelli.

Phatmama broke some tissue off the roll and blew her nose. Losing Boot wasn't part of her plans. She had it in her mind they were going to grow old together. How could her life take a turn so drastically! Coming back to prison wasn't something she had planned either. She couldn't see herself doing another bid. The type of time she was facing would keep her in prison for life. A life sentence was something she won't even try to wrap her mind around. She'd rather die than spend her last days behind a prison wall. Phatmama killed the lights in the cell by flicking the light switch on the wall. She climbed on the top bunk and faced the wall, and thought of the good times she had with Boot.

***

"Mami, I want to apologize to you for accusing you as not being loyal to the Red Bottom Squad—" Billie threw up her hand, cutting Tata off.

"No need to speak on that. In this game we must be cautious of all people that be around us. Especially that's on your team. And if it would have been the other way around and you would have been the last member to come aboard this team and all this shit would have popped off, I would have been all over your ass like a body suit!" Billie stated honestly. Her blue eyes held a deadly truth in them. Tata smirked to herself. She was feeling Billie's gangsta.

While Billie was out meeting with the lawyers and attending Phatmama and Racks' court hearing, she had Rauf check into Billie and it turned out that Billie was who she said she was.

"Thank you for being you, Billie, I mean that shit," Tata said, sitting in the leather love seat with one leg under her, twisting up a Backwood.

"It's my pleasure, babes," Billie yammered in her southern voice.

"Tata, I went in that court building today and it was no pressure on me. I mean everything went smooth as a fresh shave pussy. I even had the lawyers check and see if I had a warrant for my arrest and there was none, so I'm puzzled as to why I'm not on the police radar!"

Tata blazed the Backwood, putting a cloud of smoke in the air before she responded to Billie's question. "I'm gonna tell you why, Mami." Tata let out another cloud of smoke. She licked her full lips before she started speaking again. "Jelli don't know who you are. She don't have an address on you, she don't know your government name."

"Jelli?" Billie stated, looking confused.

"Yeah, that rat bitch tea cup got a hole in it. She spilling the tea everywhere. I hit the jail website and put Jelli name in. Lo and behold—that bitch is in their system. And check this out—she is there under murder charges!" Tata said, inhaling the Backwood and passing it to Billie who was floored by the info Tata was giving her.

"Who the fuck she kill?" Billie asked, taking the burning leaf from Tata.

"You not gonna believe this shit, Mami, while you were gone I had Rauf use his contacts to find out what they can about Jelli being over CTF. They found out that she's over CTF for killing Diego!" Billie hit Tata with the bug eye gesture, shook as hell at the news she just received. "It all make sense, Billie. Jelli must had gotten knock for Diego murder, and that bitch flip trying to save her stank ass!" Tata stated with her face all crunched like she could actually smell something that stank.

Billie was floored at what Tata was telling her about Jelli; she wanted so badly to dig a hole and put Jelli in it with half of her face missing. "So how she found out Racks' government name?" Billie asked.

"I don't know how that bitch got that info. Her and Racks wasn't even cool. So that goes to tell you Jelli been on some fuck shit long before this situation had occurred. Jelli was at that gas station when Racks dropped that police. Jelli probably was gonna use Racks' situation to get outta jail if she ever got caught up in something. Jelli probably didn't give you up because she don't know shit about you. I bet twelve haven't found my apartment yet because it's in Whip name. I'ma have Whip swing through there tomorrow to empty out my safe."

"Damn, Tata, that bitch is foul as fuck. I thought she was a stand up bitch."

"Naw, that bitch always been flakey as fuck. The only reason we started fucking with her from the get go was she was an underdog in prison. Them Spanish G-27 gang was taking those who didn't have number through ringer. In prison we learn that together we was strong, we're a mega force to be reckoned with. We lean on each other in our times of weakness. When one ate, we all ate. When we fought, we all faced our enemies together as one force. When we started to get released from prison our bond was so tight we couldn't function without one another. So when I met Rico and released his address, everyone or so seem to follow. But Jelli always try to act as if she was better the rest of us."

"So how we gonna come from under this rock we under?" Billie asked, taking a puff of the Backwood.

Tata took note of how Billie didn't exclude herself from the situation. "As of right now I don't even know, I don't even have a fucking clue!" Tata replied.

"We'll figure it out," Billie said through a yawn. It was 3:30 a.m. They had been up all day wrestling with their current drama. Both of their phones vibrated at the same time. Billie received a text from Sticks saying he was on his way to her and he wanted to play in her throat. She immediately sent him a text reminding him how much white girls love giving head.

"Daddy on his way," Billie said, getting up from the couch, heading towards the bathroom to freshen up for her brown complexioned goon.

"That was Whip saying he was on his way too." Tata started pre-rolling the Backwoods for Whip's arrival. She was hoping she could bring some peace to his mind from losing Boot.

Chapter Fourteen

"Wassup, Blood!" Whip stated nonchalantly, wondering why the man that gave him the green light to start his own set of Bloods was here in his city unannounced. No matter if he was the OG or not, it was a sign of disrespect to pop up in a nigga's city without getting permission or being invited. Whip was trying to process why Triple G was here and how he even knew to find him at Club Red Bottomz.

Triple G could sense that Whip was displeased with him being there, but he didn't give a fuck. He was the big homie that gave Whip and Boot the rank to start their weak ass line. Whip was gonna respect his five stars by choice or force. "What it is, homie? I feeling unwanted vibes." Triple G called Whip out on his bullshit. Whip looked at Kirby.

"Aye, slim, handle that business and when you do, hit Sticks on the phone and give him an update. Remember, don't fuck this up. The ball is in your court," Whip said, dismissing the new prospect. Kirby gave Whip and Sticks a pound and departed the office. He had a lot to think about, so he was gonna grab another drink, cop a lap dance from the stripper that he'd seen when he first entered the club. Whip closed the door behind Kirby. Whip walked to the wet bar and poured himself a drink.

Triple G was fuming at how Whip was really acting like he was some type of flunkie or some shit. His chest rose and fell. "Before we start you want a drink?" Whip asked, holding up a bottle of Henny.

"Naw, Henny for broke niggas," Triple G said with malice in his voice. He still clutched a bottle of Dusse in his right hand. Whip let the sideways comment go unchallenged. He calmly poured himself a shot of Henny in one of Tata's personal shot glass before he turn and confronted Triple G.

"G, I know that you receive your twenty percent for the month. So I'm wondering why you are here in my city without being invited and unannounced."

Triple G's face was tighter than a little pussy. He wasn't feeling how Whip was talking to him. He didn't give a fuck if he didn't respect the G-code and check in with Whip before he came in the city. "First, Blood, you need to check your manners and show some muthafuckin respect!" Triple G screamed; an amount of spit flew from Triple G's mouth.

Triple G stood 6'3, about two hundred and sixty pounds rock-solid. He kinda favored the well-known street fighter Kimbo Slice, but Triple was two shades lighter with a well-proportioned beard and wore a bald fade. Whip didn't let Triple's outburst faze him. He poured himself another drink before he spoke. Sticks took a seat on the office couch.

"A nigga don't mean no disrespect, Triple G, but right now isn't a real good time to be poppin up on me. I got a bunch of other shit that going on. I don't have time to babysit right now!"

"Babysit! Nigga, you got this shit all fucked up. Triple G don't need a muthafuckin babysitter or an invitation. Anywhere the bloods resides—I'm welcome to go. It seem like you need the muthafuckin babysitter. Niggas droppin' like flies under ya watch, lil' homie. What? You think a muthafucker ain't heard. You just lost your second-in-command. How the fuck you allow Boot to get caught up with a bitch!" Triple yammered, stepping farther into the office.

The statement Triple G hit Whip with wounded him. A bitterness invaded Whip's mouth. He squinted behind his thick bifocals. Whip wiped the corner of his mouth with his right thumb and index finger. "DCB loosing Boot have nothing to do with the organization. My nigga had a chick he was tied up with. She was in the game just like Boot was. She got hot. Twelve came for her. Boot bust his gun trying help his Queen escape capture."

"And you cool with that. You alright with your right hand dying about a bitch?"

"Triple G, why the fuck you so concerned with what's going on with me and my bloodline? You wasn't too concerned when you allow Spook to deny to DCB financial backing. You wasn't worried about me or Boot when you sent us back to the East Coast broke as fuck. Our ribs was touching and our knuckles were scraping the fucking ground. The same bitch that Boot die protecting was the same bitch that plug us. So don't come in my fucking city acting like you all fuckin' concerned about what going here and please don't come here speaking bad about my nigga's Queen. To disrespect her is to disrespect my nigga, Boot, and I'm not gonna go for that shit." Whip stated with a vein outlining his neck. He sat the shot glass down on the desk, giving Triple G a chance to challenge what he just spoke on. Sticks sat on the couch appalled how Whip addressed Triple G. He spoke to Triple G like he was a low-level gang member. And Triple G was accepting his disrespect like he wasn't a bonafide five-star general.

"It's clear you feel a certain way about what transpired out West! What the fuck you wanted me to do? You still got put on. Fuck what Spook was talking about. Look at cha, homie, you eating good out this bitch hands down. You got the blocks jumping, the club is thumping full of fine hoes. You still bitter about some shit that took place three years ago. Blood, you fuck that move, not me. I still kept my word regardless of the fuck up. So why we here staring at each other like we not family?" Triple G wiped his hand of over by his bald fade and held his arms out to his side. He still had the bottle of Dusse in his right hand. Whip studied his body language. Triple G's shit was off. The way his eyes darted back and forth side to side told him not to trust Triple G. And the fact that the motherfucka knew some inside details about him and DCB business was a warning sign within itself. No nigga that's claiming to be family should involuntarily seek info about things he wasn't privileged to. Whip never told him about the traps or the club. So how does he know these things if he wasn't seeking information to be on the bullshit! Whip had to play his hand smooth though; killing a high-ranking blood member could have every Blood member's guns aim at him.

Whip picked up the shot glass and poured himself another drink. "How long you staying, Triple?" Whip asked, throwing back the Henny.

"Until I'm ready to go back out West. Why? Is there a time limit on my stay?"

"Naw, not at all, blood, not at all. Just wanted to know. Welcome to DC," Whip said, raising his shot glass in the air.

A smile came across Triple G's face. He turned the bottle of Dusse up to his lips and took a swig. His head bobbed up and down with every swallow. Whip leaned over and clap this OG up, although Triple's handshake wasn't matching his smile. "Aye, blood. I got Mimi and few of my shooter downstairs turning up. Come down and join us," Triple G stated.

"Blood, I'm not gonna lie, we will chop it up tomorrow but right now I have some shit to handle. Like I said, Blood, it's bad timing but tomorrow is a sure thing."

Triple G studied Whip's face for a few seconds before he accepted Whip's decline. "Alright, but tomorrow you giving me a tour of the city."

"Well, will see about that tomorrow, but to welcome you I'm gonna let Cindy our club manager host for you. And drinks on me tonight."

"That's what's up, Blood, show a nigga some love then!" Triple yelled out. "I'm gonna get wit' the team tomorrow, blood," Triple G said, locking fingers up with Whip, shaking it up in the blood signature handshake.

"Alright, bet that up then!" Whip said, closing the door behind Triple. He sent Cindy a text giving her instruction on how to treat his guest. Then he sent Tata quick text telling her he was on his way to see her.

Jibril Williams

Chapter Fifteen

"This coke bottle glasses wearing ass nigga got me twisted the wrong fucking way. I'm Triple fucking G five star fucking General!" Triple G vented to himself as he made his way back to the booth where Mimi and his shooters were enjoying themselves. He had to wipe the grim look off his face before he made it to the booth. Mimi would pick up on his energy and become alarmed. He stopped by the bar to grab a drink and another round of bottles. Whip was acting like a straight hoe. Triple G couldn't believe that he had put him on the map and come to find out Whip got hoe tendencies. He didn't give a flying fuck what the situation out west was, and how that shit manifested; you don't treat a muthafucka of his status the way Whip just did. He was sure to make Whip pay for how he treated him. Triple G mugged Whip and Stick as they exited the club.

***

Tata peeped out the door peep hole; she held the FN in her hand. She watched Whip and Sticks get out Sticks' car and make it towards the house. "Is that them?" Billie said impatiently. She was ready to see Sticks.

"Yeah, that's them," Tata said, unlocking the door. She didn't know what to expect from Whip. So she walked away from the door and sat on the couch after leaving the door ajar. Sticks was the first one to enter the house. Billie jumped straight into his arms and wrapped her thick creamy thighs around his skinny frame. She stuck her tongue in his throat and he dug his fingertips in the backside of her plumpness. Billie ass was scrap to be a Caucasian. Sticks broke away from Billie's seduction long enough to ask Tata if she was straight.

Tata nodded and he went back to kissing his vanilla lover as he walked her to the bedroom while she was still wrapped around this body. Whip came in and locked the doors behind him. Tata sat there with one of her legs under her. She studied his face. She'd been around enough to know that something was eating at him.

"Hi, papi," she whispered.

"Wassup, Diva," Whip replied, walking over and dropping a trash bag on the table.

"What's in the bag?" Tata asked.

"Money," Whip stated, leaning over and placed three soft pecks on Tata's lips. The kiss wasn't like what Billie and Sticks shared. But it was welcoming and needed by Tata. Whip sat next to her and guided her leg across his lap. He rubbed his hand up and down her thighs, taking in her softness. The touch was welcoming for Tata. She needed to feel this form of intimacy. Whip peeled his bifocals from his face and sat them on the couch next to him. He laid his head back in the couch cushion. And Tata snuggled next to him and laid her head on his chest; she ran her hands up and down his abs through his shirt. Whip cuffed her left butt cheek in his hand. The moans of Billie started to be heard. You could hear Billie beg Sticks to go deeper. Tata and Whip both just sat there in their own thoughts listening to the love session of the couple (Billie and Stick) down the hall.

Tata was the first to break the silence between them. "Are you mad at me, baby?"

"For what?" Whip answered, eyes still close. Tata hesitated.

"For Boot," she whispered.

"That wasn't your fault, Tata. Why would I be mad at you? From the beginning I knew that you and Phatmama was going to be a problem for me and Boot. I just didn't know or foresee I was gonna lose my nigga for fuckin with y'all," Whip said, kicking his Jordan 3's off his feet. Whip's word hurled Tata but she knew that they didn't come from a place of malice.

"I'm sorry, baby, I know that I can apologize to you a million times and it would never bring Boot back and there is nothing I can do to bring him back. All I ask is allow me to be your peace. Let me help you heal, baby." Tata kissed Whip on the bottom of his chin. Her juicy lips felt good on his skin. Whip didn't respond to Tata; he just held her tighter, pulling her close. Silence fell back upon them but you could still hear Billie and Sticks moaning in the distant backgrounds.

"I went past the club and checked shit out. Cindy is holding shit down like it's her own spot. What I really like about her is when I fall through there, she gets out my way and stays out my face. She man the bar like she's a regular worker," Whip said, rubbing his hand up and down Tata's thigh and her booty.

Tata snuggled against Whip. "I'm thankful for Rauf and his people that's helping me with the club. He turned out to be a solid business partner that I can depend on. He's a little disappointed in me that I didn't get of DC and flee to Africa until this shit blows over!" Tata said, pushing her hand down the front of Whip's pants and began massaging his dick. Whip closed his eyes and enjoyed the contact he was getting from his lover. Tata went in and told him how Billie grabbed Phatmama and Racks a lawyer, and that she attended their court hearing.

Whip's eyes popped open. "Aye, Tata, I forgot to tell you that DCB got an inside man that works over CTF. He works Racks and Phatmama block where they being held at. He's supposed to take them a phone tomorrow. So you should be hearing something from them soon." Whip pushed his hand down the back of Tata's leggings, parting her cheeks; he inserted his middle finger in her gushiness.

"Sssssh! Tata moaned out. She bit down on Whip's chest through his shirt and squeezed him by the base of his manhood. Whip's piece was fighting to be released. He undid his belt with his free hand and unzipped his jeans. Tata did the honors by pulling his dick out the top of his Polo boxer briefs. Now she had access to stroke him up and down to his full potential. You still could hear Billie and Sticks getting it in. Sticks wasn't cutting Billie no slack. Her moans and screams could be heard clearly. This only motivated Whip and Tata. "You want me to suck this dick, papi?" Whip couldn't say shit; he simply nodded. Tata kissed his helmet and sucked him into her mouth and moaned. "Hummmm!" She sucked him in, wetting his dick up good before she popped him back into her mouth. She slightly blew on his wood.

"Shit!" The sensation had Whip feeling lit. He kept working his fingers in and out of Tata's wetness. This time Whip had two fingers in Tata, and they both were drenched with her juice. Tata slightly started rocking on Whip's fingers. Tata swallowed Whip, letting his head hit the back of her throat on purpose. She knew Whip liked when he touched the back of her throat. Tata didn't gag; that was for little girls trying to be a big girl. A real bitch don't have time for tears running her face and acid reflux when it came to giving head. Whip was brick up and ready to be inside Tata.

"Come on, bae, get naked. I want to be inside you!" Whip said through uneven breaths. Tata popped the dick out her mouth for the second time. Whip took control of it. He stroke himself and watched Tata get undress. She did so with the quickness. Whip scooted out the way so Tata could lay on the couch. Whip stood over her, examining her bangin' ass body. Tata's eyes were fixed on his meat. Whip pushed her thick legs back, forcing her knees to her shoulders. He got on top of her, pushing through her folds. He got to pounding Tata's pussy out and she loved every stroke. The harder he stroked her, the louder she became.

"Oh, oooh shit. Papi! Uh—Uh. Whip! Damn, Papi. Cum in me, papi, please cum in me." The dick was so good to Tata she started speaking in a language that Whip was sure wasn't her native tongue. Tata dug her nails in his back and came the hardest she ever came in her life. Her mouth was open and she shook like crazy. Tata's shaking body caused Whip to ball her into a human ball and cum deep in her womb. Whip collapsed on top of Tata. She wrapped her legs around Whip's body and came again. For that moment Whip didn't have a worry in the world. But his inner demons wouldn't rest because Triple G had surfaced in his city. But for the moment, while he could, he was going to enjoy being with Tata.

Jibril Williams

Chapter Sixteen
Three Days Later

Whip stepped out his car and adjusted the black Chanel designer jacket. He held his head up high and pushed the dark shades back on his face. His heart was in turmoil; a knot got caught in his throat. He fought like hell not to cry at Boot's viewing and funeral. But now he was at the cemetery, his tears fell with ease. He prolonged his walk to Boot's grave site. The cool breeze pushed through the fall leaves around on the ground. Winter was fast approaching. Whip sucked air in through his nose. And critiqued his surroundings. Another set of emotions hit Whip when he realized that this was the same cemetery that the little homie Gunz was laid to rest. This was the same burial grounds where he first met Tata and killed for her. Harmony Cemetery was the home of the good and the bad. The thought made Whip shake his head.

He looked over the roof of his car. DCB members stood around Boot's casket which hovered over an open grave. Pound was going live with the funeral so Phatmama and Racks could attend. Kirby was good on his word with getting a phone to them inside CTF. Whip walked slowly towards his blood nation. Though Whip wanted to hang his head to show how his heart was feeling, he couldn't because the people were watching, and he would never demonstrate weakness in front of them. Especially with Triple G sitting at the head of Boot's casket. His five shooters and Queen Mimi sat around him. Seeing them sitting there made Whip flex his jaw muscle; he was frustrated. "These muthafuckas sitting at my nigga head like they really give a fuck about my nigga," Whip mumbled to himself. Sticks saw the look on Whip's face and he stepped forward to intervene in what could turn into a bad situation quick. Whip was on his last leg dealing with Triple G. For the last three days Triple G and his shooters had been inserting themselves in shit that doesn't concern them, and Whip wasn't having it.

Sticks walked in Whip's path and placed a hand in the middle of Whip's chest but Whip knock it down. "Aye, Slim take it easy," Sticks said.

"What the fuck them niggas doing sitting there? That's me and your place!" Whip said.

"Slim, I'm just respecting my OG's. He requested to be seated there."

"Without my consent?" Whip replied, pushing past Sticks. Now resentment instantly crept in his heart towards Triple G for putting him in a position for Whip to be displeased with him. Whip was his real OG, and he valued how Whip felt about him. Sticks followed behind Whip.

Whip stood over Triple G. "Aye, Slim, you got to move and sit over there with the guests or the rest of the family." Whip pointed a finger over to where the guests were sitting. Mimi crossed her legs and squeezed her thighs together.

"Come on, blood, we comfortable here. What's the beef? We not Blood, huh?" Triple G stated.

"Most definitely you Blood. But this my homie and this my nigga here.'" Whip pointed over his shoulder with his thumb at Boot's casket that was behind him.

"And Boot's not mine?" Triple G questioned.

"Nigga, you barely knew my nigga and you barely know me, nigga. So get your ass up and show some fucking respect before I take this gesture as a sign of disrespect.

Triple G's face frowned up and his shooters stood to their feet soon as Whip's words departed his mouth. "Nigga, you screaming disrespect with all this disrespect, nigga. You got the homie in a fucking box fucking with you and ain't no one

feeling the wrath for this shit. Your whole style is disrespectful, nigga. Back out west we kill whole fucking families when
one of ours get drop." Triple G's nose flared.

"Well, nigga, this that East. If you don't like how we do it
in the East then get the fuck back out west. Until then, get the
fuck up and let me take my place!" Whip yammered.

"Triple, this not how we do shit. Let's give him his rightful
position," Mimi said, uncrossing her legs. Her tight Prada fit-
ted her just right and they displayed her v-jay-jay print. Whip
and Triple were grilling each other. The tension at the cemetery was smothering thick. The only thing that could be heard
was the leaves that blew across the cemetery grass. Mimi
stood to her feet, pulling the fabric of her pants out her creases.
She grabbed Triple G by his arm, bringing him to his feet. He
was reluctant but he allowed Mimi to escort him to another
seat. Whip didn't give room for Triple G and Mimi to pass.
They had to squeeze by him. That was cool with Mimi; she
took advantage of the situation and brushed her small breast
against Whip. Whip walked over to Boot's casket and composed his anger. He placed a hand on Boot's casket. Whip
closed his eyes and whispered: "I love you, my nigga." When
Whip opened his eyes, he nodded at the waiting preacher. He
took a seat at the head of Boot's casket and the preacher began
his recitation of his final words for Boot.

***

Phatmama, Racks and Tata wiped tears from their eyes as
they watched the funeral from their phone. Watching Boot's
casket in the ground was too much. Phatmama broke down
bad; she started pulling at her hair and crying violently. Racks
had to wrap her arm around her to quiet her. They were in their
cell, and Racks didn't want someone to hear Phatmama crying

and alert the C.O.'s that something was home. Tata was connected to them on the Zoom call. It broke her heart to hear Phatmama scream the way she did. She sat numb with one foot tucked under her, holding her iPhone in her hand and a blunt in her other hand. She watched as the last of DCB walked away from Boot's grave. Whip walked past the pound who was acting as camera man for them and told him to kill the feed. And the screen went black, but Racks and Phatmama could still be seen. Phatmama got out the view of the camera.

"Is she gonna be okay?" Tata asked.

"I hope so. She went to lay down on her bunk. I'm about to do the same in a minute. It's almost close for the C.O.'s to make their rounds and we waiting on canteen," Racks said, wiping a tear from her face with the back of her hand.

"Okay, but real quick, I forgot to mention I did some investigation. Jelli is being held at CTF," Tata said, taking a pull of her blunt. This information had Racks' attention.

"What she lock up for?" Racks replied.

"For murder and possession of a firearm. But this is the twist to the shit. She been charge with Diego's murder." Now Racks was really confused.

"How the fuck that happen?" Racks asked.

"I don't know, but I bet cha it's Jelli ass that's sitting at the table with twelve," Tata said, adjusting the phone in her hand.

"How sure are you, Tata?"

"I'm sure enough to put my life on it. She's the only one beside me and Phatmama that's still alive that knew about you murdering the police." Tata blew out a cloud of smoke.

"Fuck," Racks mumbled. She heard keys jiggling; she knew the C.O.'s were walking the tier. "Tata, I got to go. I'll be in touch," Racks said, disconnecting the call. Her head was heavy; she needed to lay down and think. She killed the cell light and crawled on to her bunk just as a C.O. was peeping into her cell and kept it moving. Racks pushed the phone under her pillow and laid there thinking about Zoey, Boot and how she was gonna repay Jelli for her betrayal.

Jibril Williams

Chapter Seventeen

DCB members had gathered at a disclosed location for Boot's repast. This was strategically done by Whip to ensure Tata's safety. The Feds were still looking for her. But she refused to sit the repast out like she did the funeral. Only DCB members were invited and knew the location of the repast, so Whip's face tightened into a ball of hate when he saw Triple G was in the building with his small entourage. Whip could feel his heart thump in his chest; it wasn't from fear. The elevated heartbeat came from rage. He watched Triple G maneuver through the crowd as if he owned the building. He locked eyes with Whip and allowed a sly smile dance across his face. His chick held the crook of his arm. She wasn't Tata but she was cold. And Whip could tell that she was hot in the ass for him. It was written all over her face. But Whip would never entertain a hoe such as Mimi. It says a lot about a woman when her man is in her presence and she still eye-fuck the next man. Whip was trying hard not to snatch the banger off his hip and push Triple G shit back. The stunt he pulled at the cemetery had him feeling like Triple G was there to shame him and try to move in on the east coast.

"Suu-Wuu!" Triple G announced as he bumped B's with Whip. At first Whip looked at Triple G's hand as if he had shit on it. But he respected the movement too much not to bump B's with him. And just like always, Triple G sensed the hesitation. "I know you still bitter about the situation at the cemetery. I bring you this as a peace treaty." Triple G smiled as Mimi handed Whip a fifth of Remy VSOP. Whip accepted and sat the bottle on the couch next to him.

"A bottle of liquor don't easily wipe away the disrespect especially coming from a man of your status," Whip stated, sipping the glass he held in his hand. The room was preoccupied with DCB members wearing red and 'RIP Boot' shirts. Some were drinking and smoking. Others were partaking in the buffet-style spread they had stationed at the far end of the room. No one seemed to be paying attention to Whip and Triple G. Whip caught Pound's eyes on them, as well as Tata's. She was in the back trying to get the overhead projector to work so she could start the slide show of Boot. Triple motioned for Mimi and his shooters to leave them.

Triple removed the bottle of Remy and sat in its place. He then sat the bottle on Whip's lap where it fell back against his stomach. Whip composed himself. Triple G was really pushing it. Triple G fired up the Backwoods he had stationed behind his ear before he started to talk.

"Blood, you acting like a nigga really had intention to disrespect. I could say the same for you by not inviting me to sit at the head of Boot's casket being that I'm the one that gave you the green light to have DCB established as an official bloodline, or I can take it as disrespectful that you didn't personally invite me to my nigga repast." Triple G said all of this in between pulls of the Backwoods; he let out a cloud of smoke. Irritation sat on Whip's face and Tata could see it from where she stood. She tapped Billie on the hip and they made their way towards Whip.

"Triple, the key word that you use was *invited*. If you not invited to something then you not entitled to it. See you thinking because you aid and assisted a nigga in their struggle that you automatic entitled to something and we both know that's not how this shit is ran. So all of that shit about you put a nigga on, yeah, that true but that wasn't all you. I got the green light from Spook as well."

"'Yeah and that nigga didn't even give you the fucking financial backing you needed."

"But your ass didn't either, nigga, and it was your fault that we didn't get it. But I didn't cry about spoiled milk, nigga. I flat footed this shit and got my money up. I didn't ask you for a damn cent!" Whip said, removing the bottle of Remy from his lap and sitting up on the couch.

"Blood, you holding them grudges like it was really my fault. I wasn't the nigga behind the gun." Triple G blew out another cloud of smoke and flexed the muscles in his jaw.

"Yeah, you wasn't behind the gun, but it was just like you was because you gave the order." Whip wiped the corner of his mouth, removing the extra moisture.

"You got me on that one. But this is not the time for this shit to even be discussed. But I'm gonna apologize to you for the way I acted at the cemetery." Triple G's apology sounded sincere. But that shit wasn't good enough for Whip.

"Nawl, Slim. You disrespected me in public. Extend your apologies to me in public."

Now for the first time tonight it was Triple G's turn to ball his face up. "Nigga, you got me fuck up."

"Triple G, you got the game fuck up."

"Damn, who the fuck is these hoes?" Triple G stated, disregarding Whip's statement as Tata and Billie walked up. He was locked in on Billie and Tata's coochie print. He tried to reach out and touch Tata and Billie's thighs. Billie was able to slap his hand away. But Tata caught him by the wrist before Triple G could make contact with her thigh, and viciously dug her nails into the skin of Triple G's wrist.

Tata hated when niggas thought it was okay to touch her. "Bitch, unhand me!" Triple G yanked his wrist out of Tata's grasp and jumped to his feet.

"Hold the fuck up, blood, that my Queen there, put that shit on pause!" Whip stated, jumping to his feet.

"I don't give a fuck who this bitch is. She don't dig her fuckin' nails into my skin."

"Nigga, you got me fuck up. You gonna respect me!" Tata said, sliding her hand in her hip where her Ruger was resting.

"Triple G, I'ma say it one more time—that's my Queen, fall the fuck back!" Whip said.

Triple G studied Tata's hand and the flare in her eyes. He was gonna comment but Mimi's presence put him on pause. If she found out that he was over here palming another woman, she was going to act the fuck out on him.

"What the fuck happen now?" Mimi said, walking up, standing next to Triple G and locking eyes with Tata and Billie.

"Ain't shit happen," Triple G said, walking away and nodding at his shooters to follow him.

The group's eyes followed behind Triple G. They watched for a second while Triple G held a brief meeting in the corner. Before his shooters exited the building.

"Whip, are you gonna introduce me to your friends?" Mimi said, sipping from her plastic cup. The Dusse had her buzzing but she wasn't drunk enough to feel the strange vibes that was radiating off Juicy Lip Diva and the supa thick scoop of vanilla that was standing in front of her.

"This is my woman Tata and this Billie—Sticks' woman."

"Hello. I'm Mimi. And Triple G belongs to me!" Mimi capped.

"Ain't no one said we wanted him!" Tata retorted.

Quickly a knavish look fell on Mimi's face.

"I'm just letting it be known that he's mine just like Whip let it been known you was his," Mimi said, taking a step closer to Tata. "But you acting like you got beef or something?" Mimi asked.

"I don't got beef. I just got the heat to cook it." Tata gave Mimi that, like: *Bitch, bring it on.*

"Whip, do you want to continue to love your woman or do you want to mourn her? Either way, I'm cool with," Mimi said, staring a hole in Tata.

"Bitch, the Red Bottom Squad don't duck no kinda rec," Billie said in her southern accent.

Mimi bust out laughing. "Cracka, please. I'ma type of bitch you ain't never dreamt about dealing with."

"Come on, y'all cool the fuck out. This my nigga repast. Respect his shit!" Whip said, stepping between the two pit bulls in a skirt. Mimi's phone vibrated in her hand. She backed away from Whip and checked her notification; it was a text from Triple G telling her he was outside in the car and he was ready to go. Mimi pushed her phone in the back pocket of her Chanel slacks and walked away without saying a word to Billie, Whip or Tata. The trio stood there watching her walk out.

"Whip, I don't like that red head bitch. What's going on her with her and the friendly ass nigga she's living to die for?" Tata asked.

"It's a long story but I will break it down to you later, this not the place. But something is up with the nigga Triple G," Whip said, walking towards Sticks.

Jibril Williams

Chapter Eighteen

Jelli closed and folded the old copy of the *Washington Post*. She got to her feet and started pacing the cell floor. She been in the hole for a few weeks now, and she was ready to get out. What she learned from reading had troubled her. She learned that Boot was gunned down by the police for trying to keep Phatmama a free woman. The news of Boot's death didn't trouble her, though. She hoped that his death caused nothing but pain to Phatmama. She hoped that Phatmama encounter the same emptiness she felt when Phatmama took Cain from her. What had Jelli all worked up was the fact the *Washington Post* spoke of Phatmama and Racks being held in CTF without bail. She knew if she would get out the hole and go back to general population, it was a strong possibility that she was going to run into one of them or even worse both of them. Jelli was really hoping that the Feds was going to come and swoop in and haul her ass off to a federal holding facility. But she could see now that the feds was dead ass serious set on her giving up her Canadian connect. Right now that wasn't an option for her. Jelli paced back and forth trying to work her problems out in her head. If she could just get ahold of Fate, she could put some shit into play where she knew would help her situation. But for right now she would just have to deal with Phatmama and Racks when she get to population in the next three days. Jelli walked over to her desk and removed her toothbrush from its cubbyhole. She found the roughest spot on her cell floor and started grinding the handle part of the toothbrush on the rough surface, filing the toothbrush down into a point.

***

Quebec Canada was cold as fuck as Fate sat in the comfy confines of a Range Rover. He still couldn't get the cold chills out his bones. The trick heat was on full blast but it did no good. Fear had sat in his bones along with the Canada cold weather. He had put off meeting with Weedy long as possible. It was either he met with the plug or the plug cut the pipeline and send his shooters.

Fate wasn't in a position to even go to war with Weedy. So he agreed to meet Weedy. Weedy had threatened his family for not protecting Jelli. He wasn't gonna allow his daughter and mother fall victim to some shit that they had nothing do with. He rode in the back seat in silence. He removed a pack of Newports from his suit pocket. He lit one and inhaled deeply and exhaled, contaminating the air in the truck. The driver wouldn't even tell him where he was going. Fate's thoughts turned to one of his stash houses being hit. He was so occupied with Weedy breathing down his neck. He couldn't give the stash house situation his full attention. It was a shame how his worker was brutally murdered. He had a group of trained-to-go shooters out there shaking muthafuckas up, trying to identify who's behind the robbery. Fate stubbed the Newport out in the ashtray when the truck pulled up into a strip mall. The driver killed the engine and nodded for Fate to get out. At that moment reality started to set in. Fate was out in a different country under the mercy of someone that he didn't know if they were friend or foe. If he was to die tonight no one would even know he was there. He boarded Weedy's private jet and flew to Canada. There was no record of him even boarding the jet. Fate pushed them scary ass thoughts to the back of his cranium and climbed out the back of the truck. Canada's cold weather wrapped around him, and he fought hard from trembling. The weather just started to break in DC, so he had gotten a taste of cold weather. But the cold he was experiencing tonight was totally different. Fate pulled the beanie farther down over his ears and pushed his hands into the pockets of his jacket, and followed Weedy's driver. In the strip mall Fate could see a few massage parlors, a couple of eateries, and a steam house.

The driver unlocked the steam house door and stepped in and Fate stepped in behind him. The establishment opened up to a small sitting area that was decorated with expensive leather chair. Fate didn't have a chance to get comfy in either of the chairs in the room before two guerilla-looking Canadians came from down the short hallway. The driver quickly disappeared out the door he had come.

"Follow me, Mr. Fate," the tall bald man mumbled. His mumble was an order and a statement all in one."

"Where is Weedy?" Fate asked, voice cracking.

"Follow me, Mr. Fate," the man mumbled again. Fate looked at the gunman who hadn't spoken yet. The man watched Fate's every movement. Fate was searched and relieved of his gun. Fate was all in now. So he followed the man while the second man trailed behind Fate, giving him uncomfortable vibes with every step of the way.

The man led Fate to a shower room and searched him again. But this time they wasn't looking for a weapon; they were looking for wires and listening devices. They made Fate strip, and he was given a white terrycloth robe. The goon pulled a small white envelope out of Fate's pocket, then opened and examined its contents.

"I need that to show the bossman," Fate announced. He handed the envelope to Fate and he tucked it in the pocket of his robe. Fate was led across the hall to a steam room. The goon tapped on the door twice before he slid it open. Fate stepped in and witnessed Weedy getting his skin flute played by a thick creamy-skinned woman between his legs bobbing her head up and down between his legs, and on a wooden bench across from them there were two women in the sixty-nine position.

Weedy waved Fate in. The goon slid close behind him. Seeing the action lowered Fate's defense all of sudden; he didn't feel like he was gonna die tonight. The steam room was hot as fuck and it almost took Fate's breath away.

Weedy let out a loud grunt, filling the woman's mouth with his seeds which she gladly swallowed without breaking her bobbing motion. She cleaned Weedy up with her mouth before he slightly pushed her head, causing her to stop sucking him off. She got to her feet and went to join the women on the bench. She started licking the ass of the woman who was on top of the sixty-nine. Whatever she was doing must have felt good to who she was performing it on. Because the woman started screaming out all kinds of "Oh baby's!" in her Canadian accent.

Weedy covered his private area with a towel before he clapped his hands twice. The three women immediately stop freakin and left the steam room, leaving the two alone. Weedy took a deep sigh. "Come sit with me, Fate." Weedy started lighting a cigar and was about pouring himself a stiff shot of some expensive drink. Fate hung his robe on a peg and took a seat next to Weedy. He put a little space in between himself and Weedy.

Weedy poured the glass of Cuvee Leonie Cognac and took a strong sniff of the drink. Weedy closed his eyes and savored the sweet smell.

"'This Cognac remind me so much of him. Strong, smooth and rich."

The statement confused Fate. But he didn't interrupt Weedy.

"The last time I sat with my comrade we shared a drink from this same bottle," Weedy said, placing the glass to his lips and taking a small sip. Now Fate knew exactly who Weedy was talking about. Weedy was talking about Cain—the man that showed him the game on a different level. Fate was with them when Weedy and Cain shared their last drink together. It was the day Weedy had offered Cain five million to take over the drug trade in D.C.

"A good man was snatched away from us, Fate," Weedy said, pouring himself another shot. But this time he filled the extra glass that was on a wooden cart that stood next to him on his left side.

"I miss my boss, Weedy."

Weedy paused from pouring the Cognac in the extra glass. "If you miss him so much then why is the people who's behind his death still have air in their lungs?"

Fate couldn't come up quick enough with a solid answer. No matter what he may have said, it would have made him look and feel like shit. Weedy handed Fate the $150,000 Cognac. Fate had then got up und retrieved the white envelope from the robe pocket. He handed it to Weedy. Weedy opened the envelope and removed a picture from it.

"What is this I'm looking at?" Weedy asked.

"Them are the bitches that helped murder Cain." Weedy easily identified Jelli except the other three women in the photo. He didn't have a clue who they were. "That's the infamous Red Bottom Squad. The crew was formulated while they were in prison. This is Tata, Phatmama—she murdered Ricco. This is Zoey. She is now deceased, and you know Jelli. I been doing my homework on these bitches. They penetrated the family. It was their goal to rob and kill Cain and steal his money. That's why Jelli was able to come up with the two million to get us back in business with you when Cain was murdered."

Weedy waved his hand, cutting Fate off. "It doesn't matter. The plug is dead. There would be no more drugs coming to DC for you."

"But—"

"Shut the fuck up and listen. The operation has been compromised. Jelli is a rat. I been ordered from the higher up to cut ties. I got an inside person that's working on Jelli's case. Jelli is going to give you up in hope she could get out of jail!"

The news made Fate scrunch his face up. "Rat bitch!" he mumbled.

"We figured if Jelli give you up, you would return the favor and give us up, and that's a chance we can't afford," Weedy said.

The steam room door opened and the same three ladies that exited the room previously were now back dressed in black, holding 9mm's with silencers.

Fate looked at them and then back to Weedy. "So it's like that, huh?"

"Nothing personal, my friend, just how the game is played when you have a multi-million-dollar business at stake or you could possibly spend the rest of your life in a prison cell." Fate knew there was no way of making it out of this situation. So he quickly made peace with God. "Fill me up for the road," Fate said, handing his empty glass to Weedy. He filled the glass to the rim and passed it back to Fate. Weedy stood to his feet and tied his towel around his waist. Fate stared down at the brown liquid in the glass for a brief second. He put the glass to his lips and downed the glass slow but steady.

"Agggh!" Fate let out from the light burn he got from the alcohol. He was ready to go now. "Hit me!" Fate yammered.

Weedy gave a nod to the woman who was playing his skin flute When Fate walked in on him. She lifted her tool and popped two shots in Fate's head like it was a common thing to do, and to her it was. She was Weedy's top killer.

Jibril Williams

Chapter Nineteen

With no hesitation the man punched in the ten-digit number to Crime Stoppers. "'Crime Stoppers—how I help you?" a woman's voice came through the phone.

"Yeah, I have information on the whereabouts of a wanted fugitive," the caller said, swallowing the dry spit that was in his mouth.

"Who is the fugitive, sir?"

"Uhmmm, Providenica Llanos. She's one of the Red Bottom Squad members. She's wanted for the jewelry store heists and murder." You could hear the computer keys being tapped rapidly through the phone.

"So you say you know the whereabouts of Providenica Llanos?" the Crime Stopper lady asked.

"'Yeah, that's correct!" the man said, watching traffic and his surroundings through his car mirrors.

"Okay, where is Ms. Llanos' location?"

"She at a family gathering. She at a repast of a friend that was murdered.

"Who's the friend?" the lady asked, trying to get much info out of the caller as possible.

"That's not important. But the location is Donovan House Lounge. You have to act fast before she leaves." The caller disconnected the call and tossed the burner out the window. He picked up his personal phone and tapped a number he had on speed dial. His call was answered on the first ring.

"What is it?"

"It's go time," the caller said before hanging up the phone.

***

"What time you think you're gonna be done here, baby?" Billie said while being embraced by Sticks. The repast for Boot had already begun to fade out. Sticks look around the room for Whip, who was seating across the room with Tata seated on his lap.

"I'mma fuck with Whip for a minute then I'm gonna come through. But it probably be late though," Sticks stated, planting a kiss on Billie's lips.

"Okay, we will be waiting," Billie stated in her southern accent.

"We?" Sticks asked.

"Yeah, me and this kitty!" Billie said with a sly smile on her face.

"Oh, is that right?"

"Uhmmm and *she* got a craving for some white thick creamy cum too." Billie ground against Sticks, feeling his dick stiffen through his pants.

"Billie, you gonna make a nigga fuck you stupid tonight."

"Good, make sure you good and drunk when you come to the spot tonight because I want you to take this ass tonight!" Billie said, kissing Sticks on the lips. Sticks' manhood really bricked up in his pants. Between the alcohol that he already consumed and the softness of Billie's body, he was ready to take Billie home and beat her pussy down like a muthafucka that stole something.

"You do know you are at a repast, right?" Tata said, interrupting Billie and Sticks.

"Well, you took your own advice because we seen how you was grinding on Whip lap. Shit, that what got us all hot and bothered!" Billie said, laughing; it was clear Billie was tipsy.

"Fuck, you was watching a bitch hard as a muthafucka!" Tata capped back. "Well, Whip got something to do. He want to go check on Club Red Bottomz before he call it a night."

"Shiiid, I want to go past the club. We haven't been past there since the opening!" Billie said excitedly.

"Girl, what are you talking about? I would love to see the club but you know it's not a safe place for me to be right now. And to be honest, I been out of hiding for way too long. I want to get to the spot and get back under the radar!" Tata stated. "I'm riding with you, Billie, so hand over the keys because your ass is lit and I'm not letting you drive."

Billie didn't hesitate to give Tata her keys. "Let me use the bathroom real quick and I'll be ready—go get the car ready."

"Okay, mami, don't be long!"

"I'm about to tell Whip I'm leaving, Sticks."

"Okay, be safe, blood," Sticks replied then stepped off to holla at someone that was getting a little too loud.

"Whip baby, I'm about to go. I will see you when you get to the spot."

"Okay, cool, baby, be safe," Whip said, standing up from the couch he was sitting on and kissed Tata goodnight.

Their tongues touched and Tata hungrily sucked on Whip's tongue.

"I love you, Whip" were the words Tata spoke when the kiss ended. Whip looked at Tata with a slight smile on his face.

"I love you too, baby!" Whip went back in and pecked Tata on the lips with his three times. He watched Tata walk out of the Donovan House. Moments later Billie was coming out the bathroom; she quickly located Sticks, said her good-byes and left out behind Tata.

Tata was already in the car when Billie came out the Donovan House. She opened the passenger door. "Oh shit! Tata,

I left my phone. I be right back," Billie said, turning on her heels and walking back into the lounge.

"Hurry up, Billie, damn, mami!" Tata complained. All of a sudden Tata felt strange sitting in the car. She felt like she was being watched. The uneasy feeling was too much; she removed her nine from her hip and clutched it in her hand while she watched her mirrors, then her thoughts went to Triple G and his stank ass bitch. "I wish these muthafuckers would try me," Tata mumbled to herself.

Tata's eyes caught in her rearview across the parking behind her two white figures sitting in their car. Their presence was screaming twelve. She could see another figure, but what made her heart drop was when she caught a glimpse of the SWAT team vehicle that was badly trying to camouflage among the smaller cars and trucks. Tata didn't wait for Billie; she smoothly eased the Audi into gear. She tapped the gas pedal and the car moved out of its parking space, and Tata casually made her way to the parking lot exit. She could see Billie coming out Donovan House and throwing her arms in the air as she saw Tata leaving her. The night around Tata lit up to red and blues, and her foot became heavy on the car accelerator, but it wouldn't be a repeat of the racing through the city with a flock of police cars chasing behind Tata. An unmarked car cut Tata's path off and another cop closed in close behind her. Tata stood on her brakes, bringing the Audi to a stop. Undercover cops were coming from everywhere. They had Tata surrounded and they had all types of weapons pointed at her. The scene made her think about *Set It Off* when Queen Latifah was surrounded by police after she took them on a high speed chase. She pushed the Audi gear into park. She grabbed her cell phone and hit Whip on the speed dial.

"You miss me already?" Whip said when he answered the phone.

"Baby," Tata said through tears, "they got me."

"'What? Who got you?" Panic could be heard in his voice.

"The police. Whip, they got me box in right outside the club. We don't have much time. Please make sure I get a lawyer. Go past my crib and make sure you get my stash. Baby, I'm counting on you to be the loyal man I know you to be."

"Tata, fuck all the preaching. I got you, baby, I'm gonna find a way somehow to get you outta this shit, baby. I promise you that."

By this time Tata could see Whip standing on the outside of Donovan House. "I love you, Whip."

"I love you too."

Tata disconnected the call. She wiped her eyes with the back of her hands and composed herself. She checked her make-up in the mirror and applied lip gloss to her lips. She knew she would be taking a mugshot tonight and she refused to be looking broke, busted. She discreetly wiped her prints from her gun and pushed it between the seat.

The police rushed the car and dragged Tata out of it. They placed her on her stomach and put a knee in her back. She was quickly handcuffed and taken away. Whip watched as the unmarked car tail lights grew smaller as Tata was whisked away.

Chapter Twenty

Seeing Tata being taken away in an unmarked police car had Whip frustrated as fuck; he balled up his hands into fists and clinched his teeth together outside of Donovan House. Whip was confused as to how twelve even knew Tata was here at the lounge. He had taken precautions for this not to happen. He waited until the last minute to disclose where the repast was going to be held, and he ordered that no one post shit on social media about the repast. Whip wanted to kill some shit. There was a leak in his organization and that wasn't sitting well with him. Whip was feeling like it was his fault that Tata was arrested. He watched a police officer search the Audi she was snatched out of. The officer quickly withdrew from the car and held the gun in the air. He cleared the gun by removing the bullet from its chambers and placed the gun in the evidence bag. Whip knew the car belonged to Billie and once they run the tags on the car she would have to have a conversation with twelve as to why there was a wanted fugitive with a loaded gun in her car.

Sticks pulled up next to Whip. "Bossman, what's the game plan, blood?" Whip let out a sigh before he spoke.

"First thing in the morning we get Tata a lawyer. Hit your cousin on the line and let him know my queen is on her way. She needs to be well taken care of. I need her to be placed in the same unit as Racks and Phatmama." Whip pushed his phone into the back pocket of his pants. Sticks was typing quickly on his phone. He was texting Kirby, giving him the rundown and his orders. "Also, Sticks, for now on it's only me and you when we talking business. There is a leak in our shit and I think Triple G is behind this bullshit."

Sticks stopped texting. "Come on, blood. I know shit ain't clicking between you and him. But this is some real rat hoe shit that's going on, if he's behind this shit," Sticks said.

"I don't know nothing about him being a rat but he's definitely got some snake in him. I can contest to that!" Whip replied.

"What's the history with you and Triple? It seems shit run deep with you two." Whip contemplated Sticks' question. He was volleying the idea if he should reveal him and the OG's history. But before he could come to a conclusion, his phone vibrated in his back pocket. He removed his phone and the answered the phone. "Hello!" Whip listened intensely. Whip quickly covered the receiver of the phone to give orders to Sticks. "Give Billie your car keys and tell her to go straight to the spot. Meet me at my car. We got a problem!" Whip said, walking to his car, listening to whoever that was on the other end of the phone.

***

Whip and Sticks pulled up on Morton Street, and police was everywhere; it was a repeat of Donovan House. But on the scene the fire department was present. CSI was present as well. They were laying down yellow number tags on the ground beside each empty shell casing that was discarded on the pavement. Smoke was coming from one of Whip's stash houses. He left a few young niggas guarding the spot. While the gang attended the repast, apparently something went wrong. Matter of fact, Whip and Sticks received other calls about their trap house being shot up and set on fire. Shit was falling apart for Whip; he needed to get a grip on shit before he lost it all.

"Here come the homie now, blood," Sticks said, watching his mirrors. Taz open the door of Whip's Range Rover and slid in the back behind the passenger seat. He went to bang b's with Whip, but his hand was ignored.

"Blood, what the fuck happen?" Whip went straight to the point. He wasn't about to play no games. Whip not acknowledging his hand offended Taz, but it also had him uneasy.

"Whip, on everything on the fucking gang—I don't even know what happened. I was upstairs taking a shit. Then all of sudden I hear gun shots. I'm not talking about no hand gun shit. Whoever it was had the sticks out or Dracos, or some shit because it was like they never ran out of bullets. When I hop off the toilet to see what the fuck was going on, the house was on fire. I tried to make it to the stash but bullets was ripping through the spot like it was Swiss cheese, then another bottle came through the window that exploded into a ball of fire. Man, blood, fire was everywhere!" Taz said with his eyes wide.

"So how you get out the house and where the rest of the homies?" Whip asked.

"They didn't make it. Whip, I had to jump out the second floor window and when I did that, there was a big nigga behind the house—he let off a few shots at me." Whip and Stick looked at each other.

Whip put the Rover into gear and left the scene. He bent the corner and stopped in the middle of the block. The trio got out the truck, and Whip led the way to the white house and before they could get on the porch good, the front door was open.

"I knew you were gonna be paying me a visit. I got everything ready for you," Ms. Hanna said. Whip gave Zoey's grandma a hug. Since Zoey's death and meeting her at the funeral, he made it his business to check in on her. Once he had a found out she lived right behind one of his stash houses, he asked her if he could place a camera on her house. The camera was pointed directly at his stash house."

"I'm sorry that I'm coming by so late but as you know I had some problems tonight," Whip said, releasing Hanna.

"'It's okay. Once I heard all the noise, I got up and made some tea and waited for you," Hanna said, closing the door behind her guests. When Hanna focused on Taz, she recognized him from the video.

"Do anyone want some tea?" Hanna asked, leading the group toward the living room.

"Naw, we good but we kinda pressed for time so can we see the video?" Whip asked.

"Sure thing, young man," Hanna said, pulling her robe tightly around her body. When she entered the living room, the furniture was like that of any other old person that lived in the hood. Ms. Hanna's furniture was covered with thick plastic.

The living room was clean with a long wooden coffee table that was stationed in front of the couch. The wall was decorated with pictures of her deceased granddaughter—Zoey. The pictures went back to when Zoey was in grade school, all the way through high school. There were even a few pictures of Zoey in her golden gloves days. Even though Whip didn't have the privilege to hang out with Zoey, every time when he visited Hanna, she had some amazing story about her granddaughter Zoey. Hearing all the wonderful things about Zoey, Whip felt like he really did know Zoey. The flat screen hung on the wall in front of the couch. It was already set to play the video. Hanna gave Whip the remote and went to the kitchen to fix her another cup of tea.

The trio stood in front of the TV when Whip pushed *play* on the remote, bringing the still frame to life but not enough for them to get a make on the car. The camera was pointing directly on Whip's stash house. Watching the video closely you could see pieces of the house being ripped from it. That's when them muthafuckas was shooting up the front of the house. There was no audio to the video. The house lit up on the screen and you could make out a fire was burning on the inside of the house. The person emerged from the car and lit what look like a bottle with a rag hanging from it. He tossed the bottle at the house. His aim was off because the bottle hit the side of the house instead of the roof of the stash house; nevertheless, the house caught fire after the bottle made contact with it. While the guy was standing there watching the house burn, he saw Taz break the upstairs window and jump from it. The screen was dark and the man could barely be seen. But once he started shooting at Taz, the spark from his gun made it easy to see his face.

"Bitch ass nigga," the trio said at once.

"Hey, watch your mouth in my house now!" Hanna said, coming back into the living room.

"Sorry!" all of them apologized.

"Aye, Whip, you got to let me handle dude. He was busting at me, blood. He tried to knock my block off!" Taz said with anger in his voice. Young blood had murder on his mind.

"You won't do nothing until I get the order. Do you hear me?" Whip replied. "We keep cool. We feed Pound misinformation and we put a tail on him."

"You still think Triple G behind this, blood?" Sticks asked Whip.

"This have Triple G written all over this shit."

"Language, young man!" Hanna scolded.

"Sorry, Ms. Hanna."

"Okay, I'm on it," Sticks said.

"'Ms. Hanna, I need a favor. Tata has been arrested. I need you to take some money to a lawyer tomorrow on her behalf," Whip stated.

Ms. Hanna's hand went to her chest where her heart was located. The hand she held her cup of tea trembled.

"No, not Tata," she mumbled.

"They grabbed her though at Boot's repast."

Ms. Hanna shook her head.

"I will do whatever you need," Hanna said, taking a seat on the couch with the hard plastic covering.

"'I'm gonna have to come past here tomorrow morning with the money and which lawyer I want you to hire for Tata. Until then try to get some sleep and come lock the door," Whip said, kissing Hanna on her forehead and leaving the house with Taz and Sticks behind him.

Chapter Twenty-One

"We came all the way on the East Coast for this bullshit. We're supposed to be out here laying low and enjoying ourselves. But you got a bitch out here squeezing trigga for your muthafuckin ass." Mimi complained as she lotioned her body down. She stood at the foot of the hotel bed with one foot up on the bed, rubbing Vaseline lotion into her thighs and calf muscles. Triple G wished she would shut the fuck up and mount him and ride his dick until he nutted deep in her walls and fall asleep. But he wouldn't dare say that shit to her at the moment. He laid in the middle of the bed naked. The sight of Mimi's naked body had him with a slight erection!

"I told you before we left I wanted to be in the streets where that action was at."

"But the shit you got going on there ain't about shit, Triple. The same nigga you gave your blessing to—you out here hating on them for no reason. This the shit that I hate about our organization. We always find a way to destroy the gang from the inside out. The gang will never grow to its full potential with this type of snake shit going on amongst us!" Mimi said, snapping the top to the lotion shut.

"Hahaha." Triple G bust out laughing. "Who the fuck made you a spokesman for the gang? You wasn't talking that shit when you was poppin the 223 round in Whip stash house."

"I did that shit for you because I'm loyal to you, nigga, fuck you talking about! I'm loyal to the fucking soil. I can't say the same for you, nigga!" Mimi yammered and slid on a pair of boy shorts and pulled a wife beater over her head. The remarks made Triple G sit up.

"Now your ass talking reckless, nothing about me is a rat."

"Ain't nobody say you were, where the fuck that come from? I'm talking about how you push upon them two bitches at the repast. What? You think I didn't see that shit? The only reason why I didn't flip out on your ass was because I'm never gonna let muthafuckas see me get outta pocket with my man because I'm just that damn loyal."

"Mimi, I know you not gonna hold me accountable for that shit. I was buzzing off the drink and I was just fucking with Whip head."

Triple G scooped his phone off the bed. He went to Facebook. Someone inboxed him. When he opened the message, the contents made his heart rate elevated. At that moment he couldn't hear Mimi talking to him. The picture had his full attention. A rat laid dead on a rat trap. The metal bar was snapped down on its neck. The picture was sent from the account of one of his foot soldiers.

"What the fuck got your attention? Triple, Triple G!" Mimi called out Triple G, before she snatched his phone out his hand.

"'Mimi, give me my phone. Who fuck you think you disrespecting!" Triple G said, jumping to snatch his phone back from Mimi but it was too late; Mimi had seen the picture and her face scrunched up.

"Why would blood send you some shit like this?" Mimi asked. Triple G knew Mimi wasn't slow; she was going to start asking some hard questions soon if he didn't come up with a good answer.

"You know how the homies be liking to play, that shit ain't about nothing." Triple G tried to downplay the situation. Mimi handed back his phone and crawled into bed.

"You and them niggas be playing some dumb ass games. That shit is borderline disrespectful. That shit is signifying you some type of rat or something. That's how a muthafucka would take that if they didn't know you!" Mimi said, slithering under the hotel blankets.

"There ain't no rat in me so a bitch would never think that about me. But ain't you gonna give a nigga some love tonight?" Triple G said as he began to massage his penis.

"Tuh. You better get that Vaseline lotion and download you some porn. Because that shit you pulled tonight at the repast got you stroking that dick tonight!" Mimi said, rolling over on her side and pulling the blanket over her head. Triple G stared at Mimi's back like he wanted to spit on her. He mumbled some bullshit under his breath but it didn't bother Mimi. He twisted up a fat Backwoods, killed the hotel lights and smoked until he fell asleep.

***

"Uhmmm! Kirby, suck it, baby, suck that coochie!" C.O. Flowers said with her legs held open wide. Kirby was down between her legs slurping her pussy with an attitude. They were on a thin jail-issued mattress in the storage room of CTF in the back of R & D. Kirby flicked his tongue across her clit, and C.O. Flowers was enjoying every moment. She had a thing for Kirby. She had pushed up on him a few times at work, but he always respectfully declined; she know it was because he favored Big Freeda. She couldn't help it that she had strong facial features. She still needed love and affection. So when Kirby came to her asking to place Providenica Llanos in a particular unit, she took the opportunity to exploit Kirby out of some head. She rolled her big hips, allowing Kirby's tongue to apply pressure on her lady button. "Oh shit, Kirby. Damn, your head fire!" C.O. Flowers moaned out. Kirby dipped his tongue in and out of her. She was so tight he had to harden his tongue and forcefully push it in to her. The thought of this C.O.'s pussy being that damn tight hyped Kirby. He unbuckled his work pants and freed his dick; it was dripping with precum. With one with one swift motion he mounted C.O. Flowers and found the opening; he pushed his head past her folds and he was in the seventh heaven. She was tight as hell. C.O. Flowers wrapped her legs around Kirby's waist, and he sank his seven inches into her. Ms. Flowers was the type that couldn't take no dick. Even the four inches Kirby pushed in her was too big for her. She was already screaming and hollering that it was too much dick for her. Kirby had three more inches to deliver. All the moaning and crying in pleasure that he was too big encouraged Kirby to slam into Ms. Flowers in and out; he found a steady pace, and it didn't take long before he exploded inside of Ms. Flowers. He laid the on top of Ms. Flowers, catching his breath. Ms. Flowers took this as though it was cuddle time for them; she reached down and stroke one of Kirby's butt cheeks.

Kirby raised his head from the crook of her neck and looked at her. Seeing her strong facial features, he became mad and jumped up and fixed his clothes. He didn't even wait until Flowers had gotten herself together. Ms. Flowers wasn't even bothered by Kirby's action; she was used to it. What Kirby didn't know was that she had been paying attention to the news and she was aware that Tata was captured and would soon be heading her way. She knew Tata was the head of the Red Bottom Squad and she had attention to have her sent to the same unit that Phatmama and Racks were both being housed. Kirby thought she was doing a favor for him, but in reality he did her a favor. She needed to bust a nut and some dick, and Kirby gave her both.

Chapter Twenty-Two

Feeling Mimi easing back into bed woke Triple G out his light sleep. The Backwoods he took to the dome had his mind foggy. He opened his eyes in time to see Mimi sliding on phone on the night stand next to bed. Triple G rolled over on his side and tried to fade back to sleep, but his thoughts started to run. He knew the situation back home was a mess. The whole team was getting popped and damn near every high ranking member of Five Deuce was being green-lighted by the Cartel—those who supplied them the work. It didn't sit well with him that Spook was still under the protection of the plug, but he was greenlighted. Triple G fished his phone from off the nightstand next to his side of the bed. He looked over and checked on Mimi. He stared at her back and studied the rise and fall of her side. She appeared to be asleep. He powered up his phone and went to Spook's Facebook page. He studied Spook's new profile picture. Normally it would be a picture of Spook on a yacht shirtless with a red L.A cap pulled over his eyes holding a bottle of Don in the air. His profile picture was now a picture of a pair of handcuffs, one forty-five hollow point bullet resting on a red cloth; the caption read: DEATH BEFORE DISHONOR.

Triple G mugged the image. He lit a Newport and blew a cloud of smoke in the air. Mimi hated when Triple smoked cigarettes especially while she was sleeping. Mimi stirred in her sleep, and tucked her head under the blanket. Triple G watched her, holding the smoke in his lungs, hoping Mimi didn't roll over and cuss his ass out. When he saw that she was still sleeping, he allowed the smoke creep out through his nose. The phone vibrated loud in Triple G's hand; it was a number he didn't recognize, so he hit the ignore button. The phone vibrated again a few seconds later.

Triple G was thinking it may be one of his hoes who was calling from a new number. He looked over towards Mimi and once he was satisfied that she was still sleeping, he hit he *call* icon button.

"Hello," he whispered into the phone.

No one responded but Triple could hear what sounded like the ocean waves crashing against the shore. "Hello," he spoke a little louder.

"You safe, blood?" the caller asked. Hearing Spook's voice, Triple G sat up in bed.

"Spook, that's you, blood?"

"Who else would it be?" Spook said calmly.

"Damn, blood, I thought them people probably had you or worse the Cartel turned on you. You know the Mexican bitches sent a hit squad to take out me and Mimi." The thought of a muthafucker to kill him and Mimi had him mad.

"That sound fuck up, but I don't think that was our friends south of our board. I think it's someone that's close to us. I think it's an inside take over, and whoever it is they snitching like fuck. Have you spoke to anyone?" Spook's question made Triple G jump to his feet.

"Fuck you saying, Blood, you calling me a rat!" Triple G got loud.

"I'm not saying shit, nigga, lower your voice when you talk to me. All I'm saying is someone is talking. I'm not necessarily saying you working with twelve. All I'm saying is you may be around someone working with twelve, but nevertheless there is a snitch among us, Blood. Where are you at? Come to me so we can put our heads together and try to figure this shit out," Spook said too smoothly for Triple G's liking. Triple G made his way to the bathroom and closed the door behind him.

"Nigga, what you trying to do? Bait me in so you can kill me?" Triple G said, dropping the lid on the toilet and took a seat on it.

"Blood, are you serious? That's how you really feel about me, homie? Killing you never came across my mind. I'm trying to help you, nigga. You get here with me and you will be safe." Triple G started contemplating Spook's words but he was still uneasy. It was like death was whispering in his ear.

"If you one hundred with me then give me your location and I'll decide if I'm gonna come to you or not," Triple G stated, taking a pull of the Newport. A long silence fell over the phone.

"Blood, not happening!" Spook's patience ran thin. "What? You trying to send twelve my way. Why, Triple G, why destroy destiny? What happen to the loyalty."

"Nigga, fuck loyalty when them crackas start talking about doing football number in the Feds, homie. When it comes to that, every man's for themselves point-blank, nigga."

"So that's how it is, huh? You just gonna rat me out, rat the gang out. Sacrifice the gang like we fuckin pawns on your chess board."

"Spook, save that shit for the judge. I'm not hearing that shit. There's no empathy coming from me. I'm not spending the rest of my life in prison for no one!" Triple G replied.

"What about your mom's life? What about Mimi?" Spook was giving Triple G a hint that his mom and woman could be punished for his action. But he knew Triple G was committed to being a rat. The Cartel wouldn't hesitate to kill everyone in Triple G's family for the shit he was doing.

"Spook, my mom have lived her life, man, and my bitch is riding out with me so send the goons—we will be waiting." Another pause fell over again.

"I never thought that it would be you to sic the Feds on me. But it was always said *keep your enemies close and watch your homies*. I made the exception when it came to you. The whole time I should have never have taken my eyes off you. I should have buried your ass when Joker and his father died."

"Hahaha!" Triple G started laughing. "I wonder what the cartel would think if they knew you was behind Joker and Mr. Rio's deaths and let's not forget the little girl." Triple G spoke through clenched teeth.

"That shit is in the past and the plug will never believe a rat. So let me say this, you rat bitch, I don't give a fuck what rat hole you run down. I will find you and murder you. You can never come back to Cali. That's on blood, nigga!" Spook yelled, and disconnected the call. Triple G stood up off the toilet and opened the bathroom door. Mimi was standing on the other side of it.

***

Spook tossed the burner phone into the ocean. He stood at the front of the yacht. His hands gripped the boat railing; he squeezed tight. A breeze off the ocean brought the smell of salt water with it. He took a deep breath and exhaled. The Cartel was relentless on applying pressure. They wanted the location of Triple G. Once they found him and have him executed, they would remove the green light on the top ranking members of Five Deuce Pirus. Triple was pop serving a UC (undercover cop). He was pop for serving two bricks. The nigga started talking soon as they placed his bitch ass in the back seat of the police car. From the Cartel sources, Spook found out that Triple G spent the weeks in their custody giving them intimate details about Five Deuce Pirus Organization. The source even said that Triple G was lucky to get the Feds a videotape of a control buy, but there was no audio to the tape.

Spook knew shit had to come together for him soon or he would be killed soon. The Cartel had him on the coast of Mexico. The yacht had been his home since the Feds started raiding traps and stash houses. Spook had twenty niggas of his crew sitting in prison, and about nine high ranking members were slain because of Triple G. He was losing on all corners. "Fuck, where is this bitch ass nigga?" Spook mumbled to himself as he looked over his shoulder at the cartel arm guard.

Chapter Twenty-Three
Two Days Later

"Have you all seen Jelli anywhere in this bitch?" Tata asked, sitting on the stainless steel toilet. Racks was sitting on the bunk and Phatmama stood posted by the cell door.

"I had Kirby look her up. She's in lockdown for a fight she had in the unit before they brought us in here. I was hoping that I could have caught her rodent ass!" Phatmama said with her face scrunched up like something stank.

"Kirby told me that she suppose' to be released out the hole tomorrow. He said it's a possibility that she could come back to this unit. If she do, I'm fucking her up on sight."

"Hold up. Phatmama, if Jelli come in the unit we got to try to finesse Jelli ass so we can all walk out this bitch," Tata said.

"Ain't no way they letting me walk out this bitch. When the genital killer case came up, they had my fingerprints on a broken glass that I left at one of the crime scenes."

"Fuck," Tata mumbled.

"So, I made up my mind I'm killing the bitch the first chance I get. I get that shit on Zoey!" Phatmama said with murder on her heart.

"I'm taking that ride with you, Phat," Racks said, standing to her feet.

"No, if I can kill her ass, you and Tata would walk. She is the only one that linking you to the police shooting." Phatmama stared, peeking at the cell door.

"I gonna ride with you, Phatmama, I'm already dying. Might as well go out with a bang, and Jelli is the reason my love is not among the earth. This is for Zoey."

"Hold up, what you mean you already dying?" Tata asked before Phatmama could get the question out. Racks' eyes filled up with tears. She lifted the corner of her mattress and removed a pill bottle. She tossed it to Tata who tried to read the name of the medication but it was difficult for her to pronounce. "Mami, what is this? What are these meds for?" Tata questioned.

Racks took a deep swallow before she spoke.

"I have HIV," she mumbled.

"No, fuck no, mami!" Tata started to rant.

"Don't do that, Tata. Don't feel sorry for me. This is the hand I was given. This how shit is and this is the story God has written for me. I live this life and this world has hurt me. My cousin Gunz was taken from me. Zoey, Boot. I was raped and now HIV. What is my purpose? Why am I here to just to suffer?" Racks' tears rolled down her face. Phatmama and Tata shared their own tears. They cried for Racks, for her pain, for her unhappiness. Phatmama walked over and wrapped her arms around Racks, and Tata wrapped her arms around them, and they shared a group hug.

***

Whip was stacking money in the safe at Club Red Bottomz. He finally went to Tata's apartment and emptied out her stash there. He didn't know she was caked the fuck up like she was. He closed the safe and secured the money he couldn't fit in the safe inside her office desk drawer. He sent Ms. Hanna the money to get Tata a lawyer. She was sitting over CTF. He was waiting on her to call him now. Kirby already called Sticks and let him know that Tata was to house with Racks and Phatmama. Whip was definitely gonna put him on with DCB's. He was putting his work in and proving to be worthy of the put on. Whip's phone rang. "Hello," he answered without looking at the caller ID.

"Whip, my brother." The foreign accent hit his ears. "Rauf, what's good? Everything is everything with the money. I counted it myself!" Whip said.

"Everything is good when it comes to that but there is some other matter that we need to address. I heard that the Queen has now been captured."

He was talking about Tata being arrested.

"Yeah, this is true," Whip said, sitting down behind the desk.

Rauf let out a long sigh.

"It saddens me to say this. Tata the Queen was the key to your success. Until further notice all business outside of Red Bottom has been placed on hold."

"Come on, Rauf, don't do this shit to me. This shit can work." Whip pleaded.

"I'm sorry but it can't," Rauf said, disconnecting the call.

"Fuuuck!" Whip yelled. His phone started ringing again but this time it was Tata. "Hello."

"Hey, papi!"

"Wassup? What them people talking about? And why it sounding like you been crying?"

"The same reason why it sound like you mad at the world," Tata replied.

"Tell me and I tell you," Whip said.

"You first," Tata retorted.

"Your little side nigga boyfriend just cut the plug on me. This nigga cut ties because he found out you was in jail."

"Don't worry, I will talk to him," Tata said, trying to calm Whip.

"Not only that, the nigga Pound is on some fuck shit. He shoot up one of my stash houses and burn that bitch down."

"What! Tata couldn't believe Pound had done some shit like that. She wondered if it was him that gave up her location to twelve. "Shit seem to be all bad, Whip."

"Shit, tell me about it. A nigga taking too many L's out."

"How you holding up? Where Phatmama and Racks?"

"They on the tier watching out while I use the phone." Tata thought about if she wanted to tell Whip about Racks' situation. But she decided against it. If Racks wanted him to know, then she would have told him.

"So what's going on with you?"

"I'm just overwhelmed. One minute I'm free, next I'm locked down like a dog."

"Keep your head, baby, I'm gonna do everything in my power to get you outta there. I got Kirby bring you your own phone. So we can chop it up at night when the jail is on lock."

"Okay, baby, thank you and thank you for getting that lawyer for me. Did you get a chance to get my money out my apartment?"

"Yeah, I just did that. It's secured in the safe. I'm gonna have to get you a bigger safe because I had to lock some of the money in the desk drawer at the club. And you know Red Bottomz haven't lost its beat. Money is piling up every day!"

"Good, I love to hear that. I just hope I can get back out there to see it," Tata said sadly.

"You will, baby, you will." Whip saw Pound walk in the club. Sticks was behind the bar. Whip watched from the camera monitors. "I got to go. I got some shit to handle," Whip said, standing up.

"Okay, baby, I got to get off this phone anyway and—oh, don't forget to feed my piranhas."

Chapter Twenty-Four

When Pound walked into Club Red Bottomz, the first person he saw behind the bar was Sticks. He threw up the b's and made his way over to Sticks. "Suu Wuu!" Pound announced when he reached the bar. "Aye, Cindy, give me a shot of Henny, no rocks!" Pound yelled.

"What it do, blood? Where you been big, dawg?" Sticks asked. This puzzled Pound because no one ever questioned his whereabouts.

"I been moving through the city seeing what's what. I heard about what happen at the stash house. Do we know who it was?" Pound asked just before Cindy—the bartender—sat Pound's drink down and walked away. He leaned over the bar and got a good look at her backside.

Sticks just studied Pound's body language. Sticks' stares had him feeling uncomfortable. He downed his drink and flagged Cindy down for another.

"We ain't heard shit about that, but we on it though. But me and Whip think it's that nigga Triple G. We ain't start having these problems until that nigga came to town."

"I don't know if he's behind that shit or not, but Triple don't seem to be too bad of a guy.

"Man, fuck Triple G. That nigga acting like a crab since he been here!" Sticks said, muggin Pound. Cindy came and refilled the glass. Pound put the glass to his lips; his hand was trembling. Sticks acted like he didn't even see the nigga's nervousness. A beautiful thick bow-legged chick that was from London came up behind Pound and tapped him on the shoulder. He almost jumped off the bar stool when she touched him.

"Oh yeah, you tense as fuck. Let me take you in the private room and take some of that stress off you," the stripper said in her London accent. He scanned Ms. London up and down. Pound licked his lips with lust in his eyes. "You sure you can stand a pounding from Pound?"

"I can take whatever pound you have to offer, love," Ms. London seductively said. Pound flagged Cindy down and told her to bring the whole bottle and another glass for Ms. London sexy ass. Ms. London grabbed Pound by the hand and was leading him to the private rooms. He stared down at London's butt cheeks; the thing she wore was doing a disappearing trick in her ass. And her bow-legged walk had Pound thinking about committing a strip club sin: *Never eat stripper pussy.*

When Pound was about to hit the private rooms' section, he peeped Whip stepping out the hall where the club office was located. Instantly the hairs on his neck stood up. *Get the fuck outta here* was what his instincts was screaming. He shook his hand free from Ms. London. He spun on his heels and started zig-zagging through the club. By the time he made it outside the club, his face was covered in sweat. He hopped into his whip and burned rubber out the club parking lot. He called Triple G on the phone.

"What you got for me?" Triple G said when he answered the phone.

"We got a problem. I need to meet with you asap!" Pound said, wiping sweat from his face.

***

The loud pack Mimi was smoking had her head heavy along with her thoughts. She sat in the hotel chair with her legs crossed, contemplating her next move. Her life was in danger and it was all because of Triple G. Last night while Triple G was snoring, she got out of bed, grabbed her phone off the night stand. She tip-toed to the bathroom. Triple G had told her not to call out to Cali, but she was missing her cousin Meesha. Meesha stayed in the streets of LA. And she kept the tea on what was poppin—where to get the exotic weed, who got shot and who's snitching. When Mimi dialed Meesha's number, Meesha was quick to tell her the rumor in the hood was that Triple was a snitch. He was telling on the whole Five Deuce Pirus. Mimi couldn't believe all the shit Meesha said.

"Cool, you better be careful rolling with that nigga Triple G. He got the whole fuckin Five Deuce lurking for his ass. It's a green light on him, girl, him and who ever that's caught with him. And I been hearing there have been some contract killers coming for his rat ass. They say the killers came up from Mexico." Meesha went on and on lacing Mimi to what was going on back home. Mimi was kinda taking it with a grain of salt but then she was thinking about how the group of goons tried to end Triple G and her life before they came to DC. She knew it was some truth to what Meesha was telling her. But it all came to light when Mimi listened to Spook and Triple's conversation last night through the bedroom door. It made Mimi's skin crawl to even think she was sleeping with a rat. She had heard it outta Triple G's mouth that he was an informant. Mimi plucked ashes from her Backwoods on the hotel floor. All the murders she committed for Triple G—and he turned out to be a rat. Surely Triple G didn't love, this wasn't nothing new to Mimi. Triple G's past infidelities had proven that. But to put her life in danger—she had to find her way out this situation. She told Triple she wasn't feeling good, that she was going to lay in and see if her sickness would go away. She was using Triple G's absence as time to think.

***

"Triple G, I'm telling you them nigga know something, blood, they was moving strange as fuck!" Pound said, pacing his apartment floor. Triple G and his goons sat around and watched Pound panicking.

"Did any of the nigga say shit to you about the stash house getting hit?" Triple asked.

"Fuck yeah. Sticks was saying he thought it was you. He was saying some shit about none of this shit started happening until you came to DC."

"Man, that's speculation, them bitch ass nigga don't know shit. If the nigga knew how to welcome a real OG in the weak ass city then maybe we wouldn't even be in this situation." Triple G and his five shooters bust out laughing. Triple G was a street nigga and in that instance his street instinct kick in. "Hold up, you came here straight from the club?" Triple G asked.

"Yeah, why?" Pound said, looking confused.

"Because them nigga probably follow—"

Boom-Boom-Boom-Boom! Yak-Yak-Yak-Yak! Bullets started ripping through Pound's apartment. Niggas was getting low, but not before Pound's head and chest opened up. Triple G's shooters were able to get their guns out; they were shooting blindly through the walls and windows. *Bloka-Bloka-Bloka-Bloka.* One of Triple G's shooters got caught up in the gun battle; he tried standing so he could get better shots off, but his body was met with brute force. Bullets tore through his body, causing him to flip over backwards. *Bloka-Bloka-Bloka-Bloka!* Triple G shot frantically while he laid on his back. He didn't know if his bullets were hitting their marks, but he kept squeezing his trigger until his Ruger was empty. His five men crawled over to his fallen soldier and scooped up his gun and started shooting with it. Triple G crawled to the back of the apartment with three of his men scrambling behind him, but one of the shooters wasn't lucky; he caught a hot one in the back of his thigh and another slug clipped his elbow. The front door of the apartment came crashing down. Sticks came in the apartment waving a Draco. Whip came behind him with the FN. They scanned the living room, looking at the damage they caused. They heard a window crash in the back of the apartment. Whip took off running in the direction he heard the crash. When he made it to the first bedroom of the right, he saw the whole window pane was broken. When he made it to the window, he could see Triple G and this shooter bend the curve leading out the alley. He could also hear police siren in the faint distance. Whip returned to the living room.

"Twelve on their way, don't play with them, kill them!" Whip said, mobbing past Sticks.

Sticks quickly raised the Draco. *Yak-Yak!* He popped Triple G's shooter. Just to make sure everyone was dead, he gave everyone on the floor a head shot and quickly disappeared out the door behind Whip.

Chapter Twenty-Five
Four Hours Later

Whip and Sticks were laying low at Tata and Billie's hideout spot. Billie came in and served them some drinks. Ever since Tata's arrest Billie hadn't left the house. Billie paid a lawyer because she learned that the Feds was looking for her for harboring a fugitive, because Tata was caught behind the wheel of her car. As for the gun that was found, the gun was registered to her. The lawyer told her that they could work something out and have her turn herself in and post bond immediately after. But Billie wasn't ready to turn herself in to nobody's jail. She told the lawyer to work the details out but she had no intention of turning herself in. Seeing Billie made Whip think of Tata and missed her. He was wondering if she was alright. He was waiting for Kirby to give Tata her phone so he could face-time with her. He needed to see Tata's face. Billie left the room and left Whip and Sticks to themselves.

Meek Mills' *Blue Notes* played out the Alesia speaker. The TV was off and Sticks sat up in his chair and started breaking buds up on the coffee table so the weed could be rolled up. "Aye, Whip, let me ask you a question, Blood."

Whip unrolled a piece of Backwoods and dumped the tobacco in the ashtray and replaced the Backwoods' contents with thick buds of the loud pack. "Speak your mind, Blood," Whip stated as he started twisting the Backwoods.

"What the story behind you and that nigga Triple G? It's like the tension was already in the air between you two when he walked in the club office?" Whip took his time flipping Sticks' question over in his head. Whip cleared his throat.

"A few years ago. When we very first started out with DCB when it was just me, Boot, Racks, Gunz and you. You don't know this but the nigga Triple G reached out to us on

FB. He was looking to put some niggas on in DC. He flew me and Boot out to the motherland of gang land. Cali was a culture shock for us. Me and Boot. He was on the east coast fakin' like we was bloods, when they was out there living that shit for real. We got put on for real. We were jump in the gang, me and Boots. That shit made our bond so light, coming outta that shit official bloods." Whip put some heat to the Backwoods he just twisted up. He blew a cloud of smoke into the air before he continued to talk.

"The plan was to make a hit for Triple G and a nigga named Spook. Spook was like the ultimate G or some shit. He had that shit on lock out West. We didn't see much of the big homie. But his presence was felt. Triple G and Spook sat us down at the table and asked us how far we trying to nail this blood shit. I told Spook that I wanted to start my own bloodline. I wanted my own stamp in this bloodline. I didn't want to be under no other blood organization. It was DCB or nothing. At the time Spook and Triple G respected my ambition, but they were really concerned about my gangsta. The deal was if we hit some important people we would be put on and Five Deuce would give us the financial backing to grow our bloodline. I'm talking about money, guns and product, but shit didn't go as planned. We was told not to kill none of the children, that was Spook's words. We were suppose' to hit some Mexicans by name of Joker and his father Romas. The hit went sweet. Joker and his dad got the haircuts every two weeks at the same barbershop. This particular week the black Maybach pulled up to the barber shop, then Joker and Romas went in." Sticks listened to Whip tell his story. The way Whip was telling his story was so intense. Sticks took a sip of the Henny Billie made for them and lit his own Backwoods. "We was dressed up as women, blood, we watched Joker and his father from across the street. We blinded by sitting at the bus stop across the street. When they came out of the barber shop, me and Boot bump our B's together and we put on for set. We pushed across the street. Joker or his dad didn't even see it coming. I slid up on Joker and drop four in his head. Boot took pops out with two head shots. Boots was standing over Romas, making a mess of him by emptying bullets into his body. Suddenly the back door of the Maybach opened up and a woman came out blazing her guns. After she got a few shots, she barely missed Boot. When I was shooting, a couple of stray bullets hit the back passenger car. We got the fuck outta there. When we made it back to Spook and Triple G, we learned that there was a child in the back seat of the Maybach. She caught two of my slugs to the face. Spook went in on our ass. Triple G failed to tell us that the father's girlfriend always roll with them to the barber shop. This particular day the girlfriend's daughter was with them. Spook went back on his word of financially backing us. Spook threatened if we the ever came back to LA again he would have us bodied." Whip relit his Backwoods. He did so much talking it went out.

"Damn, blood, that's some wild shit there. So who the fuck was Joker and Romas?" Sticks asked. Whip looked at Sticks.

"Romas was Spook pops and Joker was his half-brother. Romas favored Joker over Spook because Spook mother was black and Joker mother was a hundred percent Mexican. Romas was tied into the cartel. That's why they call Spook, *Spook.* He was black and half Mexican."

"Shit! That shit is deep, Whip," Sticks said.

"Not deeper than the grave I'm trying to put Triple G ass in," Whip retorted, taking a hit of the Backwoods. He was disappointed in his failed assassination attempt on Triple G. He knew he should have waited until Triple G and his shooters came outta Pound's apartment, but his adrenaline was pumping and his impatience influenced him to go Rambo on mission, causing him to miss his marks. Before Sticks could reply to Whip's comment, the phone vibrated on the table. It was a text from Cindy saying someone shot the club up and set it on fire.

Chapter Twenty-Six

When Whip and Stick finally made it to Club Red Bottomz, the fire department was already there and they had the truck water hose spraying down what used to be Club Red Bottomz with gallons of water. Metropolitan police department was there trying to find a witness. The club and half naked strippers stood around crying and traumatized from the event. Whip saw Cindy in the crowd trying to console Ms. London and a group of strippers he never saw before. It must be their first night working the club. When Cindy saw Whip approaching, she broke away from the group.

"I'm sorry, Whip, but this is too much for me. I'm having Rauf come to get me!" Cindy blurted out. Whip grabbed her by her arm and escorted her to Sticks so they could talk in private. He got in the passenger seat. Sticks was behind the wheel and Cindy crawled into the back.

"What happened?" Whip asked. Cindy took a deep breath and
and balled her hands into fist.

"I was working the bar like I always do. Then I heard a loud pop. When I looked up, there were two or three gunmen in the club just shooting shit up. Then I hear glass or bottles breaking, then what smelt like gasoline was in the air. All of a sudden the club was on fire." Cindy started to cry.

"Was anybody hurt?" Whip asked.

Cindy moved her head up and down. "No one was killed, thank God, but a few people was shot."

"When is Rauf coming to get you?"

"He wouldn't say. He told me to just sit tight and he will be here," Cindy stated, wiping her tears away with her shirt.

"Can we take you home?" Whip asked. Cindy had always been good people ever since Rauf introduced her to Tata. Rauf claimed that Cindy was just there to help Tata run the club until Tata was able to run the club efficiently, but Whip felt she was there to keep tabs on Tata. Whip wondered, *Was this how Rauf knew Tata got arrested?*

"No, my car is parked right over there."

"Okay, if you need anything you have my number," Whip said. Cindy nodded and got out the car.

"What you think, boss man?" Sticks inquired.

"This got Triple G name written all over this shit. We need to find this nigga asap." *Vrrrr, Vrrr, Vrrr!* Whip's phone vibrated. It was a number he didn't recognize but he answered it anyway. "Hello."

"Hey, Papi, it's me," Tata said in a whisper. Soon as Whip heard his Queen's voice, he thought about all her money that was lost in the club fire.

***

Hot tears rolled down Tata's face as she watched the live feed of her club being burned to the ground, and the fact Whip told her that all her money was in the club sent her numb. She wanted to die. She couldn't take it no more. She disconnected the call and tossed the phone on her bed bunk. She was in the cell by herself and she was thankful for that. At that very moment she became angry with God. She didn't understand why God always wanted her to carry the burden. She'd been to prison. Now she back facing life, her business burned to the ground along with money. A companion turned rat—that's what Jelli was, Tata thought. She now what knew how Wayne Perry felt when Alpo ratted him out. She was back at square one broke and back in jail. Tata broke down and fell to the floor. She cried her eyes out and cursed God at the same time. *Vrrrr! Vrrr! Vrrrr!* Tata heard the phone vibrate. Being in the cell by herself the phone seemed to vibrate louder than it normally would. Tata didn't want to talk with Whip right now, but she answered the phone anyway.

"Hello!"

"Aye, man, tighten the fuck up. I can hear your ass all the way over here." Phatmama's voice boomed through the phone. Tata wiped her tears away with her hands. "I got word what happen from Billie about the club. But that shit fuck all the way up, but we Red Bottom Squad—we come strong even when we weak. Don't let the circumstance of the situation break you. We have to formulate a plan, Tata. There's no time for tears. We can cry all we want when we sitting in prison for life. We got to keep that same energy we had when we was robbing and killing. We got to find a way to keep this Red Bottom Squad alive."

"But the club—"

"Fuck the club. We can get that shit back and ten more like them. But right now we got work to do. Let's plot and strategize. This shit don't stop for this here! Tata, I love you, girl. We can do this. We have all the tools to come in from under shit." Phatmama's words made Tata stop crying. She was listening intensely. She was gaining strength from Phatmama's words. She didn't know what Phatmama had planned, but she could hear conviction in her voice and Phatmama always rolled with her if she was right or wrong on all situation. So she would do the same for Phatmama. "Tata!"

"Yeah!"

"Get some rest. We start planning tomorrow. And we stand firm on the Red Bottom Squad Motto: If one ride—" Phatmama said.

"We'll all roll." Tata replied.

"If one hesitate—" Racks chimed in.

"Then we'll all motivate," Tata recited.

"And if one betrays—"

"Then know God forgives, and we don't!" all three women said in unison. Tata disconnected the call. She felt charged and ready to pick the Red Bottom Squad up off its knees.

Chapter Twenty-Seven
Seventy-Two Hours Later

"What type of bullshit you on, Mimi? Put this dick in your mouth." Triple G was frustrated Mimi wouldn't give him no play. She wasn't coming up off no pussy, no head. Shit. Mimi wasn't down to give him a hand job. He stood in front of Mimi with a limp dick dangling in her face.

"Move the fuck outta my face, Triple, and I'm not telling you no more."

"Or what, bitch? This my pussy. That's my throat and I want some. So break bread or play dead!" Triple G said, taking the palm of his hand and mushing Mimi's head back; the force of the push sent her flying back on the bed she was sitting on. Her legs flew open and Triple G dived between them. She tried to fight him off, but he was way too big and strong for her to do so.

"What you gonna do? Rape me? Get the fuck off me, Triple G!" Mimi screamed. The heat from Mimi's coochie was hot. And it made him brick up, her little ass looking good as fuck in the red Vickie thongs set the she had on. It's been three days and Mimi has been giving him the cold shoulder. She been in and out the bathroom talking on her phone off and on. When Triple G tried to ear hustle on her conversation through the bathroom door, it was hard to hear what Mimi was saying and who she talking to because she always turned the sink faucet on. All Triple G could hear was running water.

"Come on, Mimi, just let a nigga put the head in, come on, be still." Triple G forced the crotch of Mimi's Vickies to the side and strong-armed two fingers in her love box; the slickness of her walls excited him. He wanted to be inside Mimi.

He didn't know why Mimi was denying him. This was something she had never done before, but he was gonna make it his business to make sure she'll never do it again.

"Stop! Triple G, get the fuck off me!" Mimi yammered. Because she was on the verge of tears, Triple G could tell she was mad.

"Don't cry, baby, just give ya nigga some," Triple G said, removing his finger and freeing his dick; he was thick and hard. The head of his dick was dripping with precum. He spread Mimi's legs open with the weight of his body, and inserted himself inside of her. Mimi was naturally wet no matter what was going in her life. Mimi was a snug fit. Triple G only got half of his wood in her before he had to pull out the head and push back down into Mimi. Tears fell from Mimi's eyes.

"No, baby, don't cry, baby. Don't cry," Triple G whispered, leaning forward, kissing Mimi's cheeks and tears. Once the base of his pelvis fell against her softness, the sensation was so dissolving, it made him rest his face against Mimi's and started humping away. Mimi took advantage of the situation; she bit down on Triple G's face with everything she had in her. Mimi's teeth sank in him like butter. "Agggh! Agggh!" Triple hollered and brought his thrusting to an end; he pulled out of Mimi but Mimi wouldn't let go. Triple G grabbed her face and Mimi's teeth sunk deeper. "Get the fuck off me, bitch!" Triple G's hands found Mimi's neck and squeezed. Mimi clawed for his eyes, causing him to let go of her neck. Mimi finally let Triple G loose; a good chunk was missing from Triple G's face. Mimi spitted the chunk out on the bed. Mimi scrambled to recover her Mack 12 that was located on the dresser. Once she did, she cocked it, putting one in the chambers. Triple G froze hearing Mimi's weapon cock. He held his face where Mimi bit him. He knew Mimi would cut him down with the gun if he made a sudden move.

"All of this about some pussy?" Triple G questioned, breathing hard.

"No, it's not about the pussy. It's about me not fucking a low life ass rat!" Mimi said, holding both hands with the Mack. She had it pointing dead at his chest. The look in Triple G's eyes asked the question of how did she know. "I found out from you, you told me. I heard you talking to Spook the other night." A knock came to the door. Triple G was starting to think that his shooters heard all the commotion in the room since they were just next door. But when she still held him at gun point, skillfully maneuvering to the door without taking Triple G out her sight, he knew something was wrong. Mimi opened the door and in came Spook and Whip. Triple G's breath got caught in his throat. Spook didn't say a word; he just made eye contact with his erstwhile comrade. Whip held a blue steel 357 with a silencer on it. Triple G badly tried to swallow the lump that was formulated in his throat. Two Mexicans came into the room and closed the door behind them. Mimi quickly put her clothes on. Mimi had reached out to Spook, letting him know where Triple G was holding up at. She told him about the shit he was doing to Whip. At first, Spook was apprehensive. Once Mini convinced him that she was loyal and stood firm with the Five Deuce Pirus, they devised a plan. Spook reached out to Whip and they sat down and hashed out their differences about the situation that happened back out West since Rauf pulled the plug on Whip. Whip told Spook that he would give great thought on letting him supply DCB. So all they had to do was handle Triple G.

"Why, Triple G? Why? I never thought it would be you on the end of the rat trap," Spook said.

"Man, do what the fuck you gotta do. I ain't begging for my life!" Triple G said. Silence fell over the room before Spook spoke.

"Very well, give it to him." Whip raised the 357 and squeezed two slugs off into Triple G's chest, causing him to fall back on the bed. The two shots could barely be heard due to the silencer that was on Whip's gun.

Spook fished his phone out his pocket, hit the camera on the phone and started recording; he made sure he didn't get no one on camera except Triple G's face. Members watched the live feed, back in Mexico. Spook removed a knife out his pocket and a pair of pliers. He walked over to Triple G's dying body. He stuck the pliers in his mouth and clamped them on his tongue, and pulled upward hard. He looked dead in the camera and spoke in Spanish. "La lengua de una rata" which meant: *The tongue of a rat.* Spook then took his knife and hacked Triple G's tongue from his head. He then placed the tongue in a thick red cloth and placed it in his back pocket. Whip killed the camera. Spook nodded at the two Mexican men and they quickly went to work. They quickly moved Triple's body to the bathroom and put him in the bath tub. The two men were Spook's cleanup crew. They were going to dispose of Triple G's body once they gut him and his three shooters that were already murdered in the hotel room next to them; it would be like they never even existed.

"I really appreciate you accompanying me on this mission. May
we all be granted peace since the rat is dead," Spook said, stopping at the back of his all-white Maybach with its red rims.

"We all should rest well now," Whip replied. He felt uneasy around Spook. He always had that effect on Whip. Spook favored the rapper *Game*, but Whip was far from being afraid of him. Spook opened the back of the Maybach and reached and removed a small duffle bag, and handed it to Whip. Whip sat the bag in the truck and opened it.

"What this?" Whip asked, looking at the stack of money.

"That's the financial backing money I owed you," Spook said, smiling. He bumped B's with Whip and hopped in the back of the Maybach. He removed the tongue from his pocket and dropped it a champagne bucket of ice. Mimi nodded at Whip, crawled into the back of the Maybach and closed the door. The window came rolling down. And Spook poked his head out the window. "Don't forget to consider my offer; there's a lot of money to be made," Spook stated. Whip nodded. Then a thought came to him. And he stopped Spook before he could roll his window all the way.

"Aye, Spook."

"What's up, Blood?"

"What you gonna do with the tongue?" Whip asked.

Spook shrugged. "Fuck if I know. The cartel wanted it." Spook laughed and rolled the window back up. The Maybach backed out of the parking space and just like that Spook was gone.

Jibril Williams

Chapter Twenty-Eight

Jelli was laid back on her bunk reading an old *Washington Post*. She was excited to learn that Club Red Bottomz was shot up and burned down. She read how Tata was captured at Boot's repast. She was so happy that all them bitches was in jail. There was an article in the open paper that had Tata, Phatmama and Racks attached to it. The article spoke about how they were the infamous Red Bottom Crew that were robbing jewelry stores and banks. The post said the Red Bottom Crew went on a six-million-dollar robbery spree. Jelli didn't think the paper was accurate about that, but Jelli did know they were getting it in. The paper was even talking about how the all-woman crew was tied in to killing DC Kingpin—Cain Boss. Jelli didn't know where the *Washington Post* was getting the info from, but they were hitting the nail on the head.

"Roberts, Roberts!" Jelli could hear the C.O. calling her name. She got up and stuck her head out the cell door.

"Yeah."

"You have a legal," the C.O. said at the front of the tier. Jelli dipped back in her cell and got herself together. She looked into the acrylic mirror, making sure she had nothing in the corner of her eyes. Jelli had been out the hole for two weeks now. She was housed in B unit across the hall from Tata. She grabbed her legal folder and she was ready to go. Five minutes later, she was seated in front of her lawyer. "How are you, Ms. Roberts?" Ms. McNeal asked.

"I'm good. Any news about me getting out this place? Cos a bitch could really use a day at the spa right about now." Ms. McNeal didn't find Jelli's little joke serious. So she held no cut cards with Jelli.

"I'm sorry to tell you this—you won't be going no time soon unless we beat this trial."

"Trial? Ain't no one going to trial. What about me giving up The Red Bottom Squad and Fate? What about that?" Jelli asked with attitude. She was tired of sitting in jail and she was ready to do anything to get out.

"Well, the same Superior Courts are willing to work a deal with you on the Red Bottom Squad deal. But the Feds backed out of the deal with Fate," Ms. McNeal said.

"And why is that? They are the ones that have the hold on me, right?"

"Yeah, you are right but here is our problem." Ms. McNeal removed a Canadian newspaper article, the title of which read: *Jerome Fate Fuller Found Dead in Canada.* That's all Jelli could read before anger took control over her.

"Fuck that! Tell the Feds I want to make a deal. I will give them the Canadian connect. They want Weedy. I will give them him on a silver fucking platter!" Jelli yelled.

Ms. McNeal looked at Jelli with disgust all over her face. But she held her composure.

"Ms. Roberts, are you sure you don't want to go to trial? We can beat this." The lawyer pleaded, trying to talk some sense in Jelli's head.

"Fuck no! Get me the Feds over this bitch. I'm tired of playing games. I want out now!" Jelli yelled. Her voice echoed through the visiting hall. Her lawyer shook her head and gathered her belongings. "Okay, Ms. Roberts, the Feds is what it is," Ms. McNeal said, standing to her feet. She dug in her bag and removed a pack of gum and slid it to Jelli. "Here, some gum. I will be back in a few days after I talk with the Feds," Ms. McNeal said, walking out the legal visiting room. Jelli snatched the pack of double mint gum off the table and placed it in her legal folder. Walking back to her unit, she was mad as fuck that Fate was murdered and she was stuck in jail.

She was definitely going to use him as a means to get out of jail, but fuck it! Weedy would do.

Flipping the situation over in her head, by the time Jelli made it to *B Unit*, she was madder than what she was when the lawyer told her she didn't have a deal. The C.O. standing in the control booth hit a button on the panel to let Jelli in the unit. Jelli went straight to her cell. The unit was active with females playing spades, checkers and other board games to kill the time away. Others utilized the phones that was stationary on the walls of the unit. When Jelli made it to her cell, her celly was occupying the cell; she was in there with a picture of Drake. She was laying on the top bunk with legs open and hand down in her jumper. She was staring at the picture with lust in her eyes; you can tell Mona was in there and fingering herself. When Jelli opened the door and walked in the cell, Mona jumped quickly and removed her hand from her jumper. "What's up, Jelli?" Mona said, climbing down off her bunk and started washing her hands.

"Ain't a fuck thang going on. I'm still stuck in this bitch!" Jelli said with attitude.

"Jelli, listen, you got a murder. You gonna be over CTF for a while fighting for your freedom. Look at me—I been sitting for the last two years. Shit like this take time." Mona dried her hand.

After drying, she gave Jelli real facts on fighting a murder charge. Mona was facing murder charges. She had killed her best friend for sleeping with her boyfriend.

"I know the process. But some shit happen in my case that was supposed to send me home, and this shit isn't happening fast enough!" Jelli complained.

"Well, it's gonna happen soon or later, just stay positive," Mona encouraged. Jelli didn't want to hear that shit but she held her tongue. The legal folder slipped out Jelli's hand; the legal documents hit the floor along with the pack of mint gum.

"Fuck," Jelli mumbled. She didn't want to share with her celly but now that Mona had seen it, she had to at least offer her a piece. "You want some gum?" Jelli asked after putting her legal documents back in her folder.

"Hell the fuck yeah," Mona said seriously. Jelli popped the pack and gave Mona a stick of gum. Jelli and Mona's cell door came open. Mona saw the unit C.O. at their door with a Lt. Mona deceitfully dropped her piece of gum in the toilet.

"Ms. Roberts, pack your bags, you being moved," the Lt. said firmly.

***

When Ms. McNeal made it to her car, she called on her phone.

"Hello, love," a smooth voice said over the phone. Ms. McNeal blushed hard.

"Hey, baby. Ms. McNeal cooed into the phone.

"How did it go?"

"Weedy baby, that bitch is a bonafide rat. Once I showed her that Fate was dead, she immediately informed that she want to make a deal with the Feds to rat you out!" Ms. McNeal stated with distaste in her voice.

Weedy and Ms. McNeal had met through Cain a few years ago. They sexed off and on. Ms. McNeal didn't want to end her career as a lawyer to be with Weedy, and Weedy wasn't ready to give up the gangsta lifestyle. But Weedy's lifestyle had Ms. McNeal hooked. When she was hired and got in the case, she knew that Fate worked for Cain and Cain worked for Weedy. So she reached out to her long distant lover.

"I'm sure you gave the rat the cheese?" Weedy asked.

Ms. McNeal giggled. "Yeah, I gave the bad breath bitch the gum. She'll be dead by tonight."

"Very well. When are you flying out, my love?" Weedy asked.

"Tomorrow morning and I'm coming pantiless," Ms. McNeal
replied, blowing a kiss to Weedy through the phone before she hung up.

Chapter Twenty-Nine

"How shit looking in there, Tata?" Whip asked with concern on his face and in his voice.

"Everything is everything, papi. Why you keep asking that, why?" Tata asked, staring at the screen of her phone. She was facetiming when she knew she should not be on the phone during the day. It was almost lunch time and it was during this time of day that the C.O.'s liked to walk and make their rounds. Especially the male C.O.'s—they knew most of the women on 'A Block' liked to take their showers right before lunch. The officers would catch them getting out the showers and catch an eyeful of titties and ass, or they would get real lucky and walk up on one of the women lotioning her body in the cell.

"I'm just asking, baby, that's all. What? A nigga can't worry about you?" Whip said, smiling. Tata smiled back.

"Yeah, I guess you can," Tata said, blowing a kiss at him. Whip got real serious.

"I miss you, Tata, I really wish that you wouldn't be there when shit go down. There is no need for you to be. I'm sure that Phatmama is very capable of handling business.

"Whip, Phatmama is my fuck girl. This probably be the last time I will see her and I need to see Jelli ass get what coming to her." Two taps came to Tata's door, and Racks walked into Tata's cell.

"Girl, get off the phone. The Lt. and a C.O. just came on the tier!" Racks said.

"Bye, baby," Tata said, disconnecting the phone and stuffing her phone in her panties and walked out the cell casually. She was nervous seeing the Lt. approaching her. "Ms. Llanos, pack your belongings, you being moved!" the Lt. said firmly.

"What! Move where? What I do?" Tata protested, asking question after question.

"You moving to *B Unit*," the LT said sternly. Tata looked confused. She didn't have a clue to what the fuck was going on. She had learned from Kirby that Jelli was in B unit. Her moving was gonna fuck up their plan. "Listen, you don't have all day. Pack your shit!" the Lt. demanded. Tata stared at Phatmama and Racks; they were quiet about the current situation. They couldn't even look at her. Tata wondered what was the fuck going on. She looked over the Lt.'s shoulder and couldn't see who was working the bubble. Kirby did come to work the next shift. The move they been planning was to take place tomorrow. This frustrated Tata. She went in her cell and quickly packed her shit. She threw everything in the sheets that was on her bed. She didn't have much but a bunch of commissary. She tied the ends to the sheets and threw the bundle over her shoulder.

Phatmama was standing there with Racks. The girls quickly hugged Tata. "I love you, Mami. It was a pleasure and a helluva ride," Phatmama whispered in her ears. Racks hugged Tata tight. Tata could feel the bulge on Racks' waistline. Now she was really confused. All the women in *A Unit* stared and watched the Lt. and C.O. escort Tata out the unit.

"Lt., why am I being moved?" Tata asked.

The Lt. looked at her with a smirk on her face. She often see this in the jail. An inmate put a request in the box stating they feared for their safety. When it's time to move them, they act like they don't know what's happening, trying to save face with the other inmates. She looked at Tata. "We got your request to be moved because you are afraid for your safety in *A Unit*," the Lt. said, and signaled the control booth to open the sally port. When Tata saw who was in the sally port, she couldn't reply to what the Lt. told her about the request. Her eyes fell on Jelli, and Jelli was just as surprised to see her as well. The C.O. started processing Tata in.

Tata looked at Jelli with hate in her eyes. "God forgives— we don't," Tata mouthed to Jelli, reminding her of the last part of The Red Bottom Squad Oath.

"Fuck you," Jelli mouthed back.

"Rat bitch, Tata mumbled. The exchange of words was so brief the Lt. didn't even notice. Tata stepped out in the hallway and a block grill closed behind her. She looked over her shoulder as Jelli was walking into *A Unit*, being released to the savages that were waiting on her.

***

Jelli stepped into *A Unit*. The unit seem chilling quiet. Jelli lugged her belongings to her cell and took the unit's silence as no threat. The last time she was in *A Unit*, she had to beat a bitch ass. Then Jelli started wondering: *Is Tata in the unit spreading the word I'm a rat and is that the reason for the unit's silence?* Jelli wasn't stunting the bullshit though. She would be quick to fuck one of them hoes up for stepping to her about her business. Jelli stepped in her cell and slid the door close behind her. She threw her belongings in the bottom bunk. *I'm going to be living by myself for a few days*, Jelli thought to herself. Jelli looked around the cell. Even though it was fairly clean, she still felt she needed to give it a Jelli cleaning. She wanted to do that before she started unpacking. Her thoughts went to Tata briefly then the question of where Phatmama and Racks were being housed. When she walked out her cell, her question was answered when she was met with Phatmama and Racks' angry faces. Fear instantly jumped in her body; Phatmama and Racks could smell it like a pack of wolves could smell it on their prey. Jelli tried to run, but Racks popped her in the jaw with a hook. Fear paralyzed Jelli's legs; they were wobbly and she couldn't get her balance to stop her from falling when Racks cracked her in the jaw. Phatmama kicked Jelli in the face. The inmates heard the commotion in the unit and ran to see what the fuck was going on. Day-to-day life in jail was so boring they took pride in watching someone get their ass beat.

Jelli's nose snapped when Phatmama's foot made contact with it. The C.O. in the control booth watched the whole event unfold. She hit her emergency button, calling all available officers to *A Unit*. Jelli tried to get to her feet but she was dizzy. A sharp pain exploded between her ribs. She fell back on the floor and saw Phatmama standing over her with a knife in her hand. She touched the ribs, and her hand came back covered in blood. The sally port doors opened up and C.O.'s rushed in. Racks removed the high point 380 from her waist and let a round off in the air. The gun echoed so loud in the unit it made the C.O.'s and inmates run for cover. Racks pointed the gun at the C.O.'s that were overwhelmed with surprise that an inmate had a gun in the building. "Don't fucking move!" Racks yelled. Horror was in the eyes of everyone; they didn't know if they were going to live or die that day.

Racks stood between Phatmama and the C.O.'s just like they had planned. Phatmama was merciless on Jelli. She stabbed Jelli repeatedly. "You rat bitch!" Phatmama screamed. "This for Zoey, this for Boot and every muthafucka you ever done wrong to." Phatmama continued to stab Jelli. Jelli was bleeding out bad. She was becoming light-headed and she could no longer fight Phatmama from stabbing her. She laid there with her arm to her side. She couldn't hear the cries of the other inmates in the unit or the commands of the C.O.'s telling Racks to drop the gun so they could get her some medical attention. All she could hear was her shallow breathing and the thumping of her heart. She briefly wondered why she was dealt the hand she was dealt. Phatmama rolled Jelli onto her stomach and took a seat on her lower back. Phatmama leaned forward and whispered in Jelli's ear: "God forgives. The Heart of a Savage don't." Phatmama gripped Jelli by her hair and dragged the blade of the knife across Jelli's throat. Jelli's body shook as death took over her body. The C.O.'s looked on in horror. Phatmama slammed Jelli's head forward into the floor, causing a loud thump.

Phatmama got to her feet and wiped her bloody hands on the pants of her jumper. "Lockdown, this is an emergency—a lockdown. All inmates report to their assigned cells. Lockdown!" the voice on the loud speaker announced but no one in the unit moved. They were too terrified to do so. Racks' hand shook with the gun in it; she still held it pointed at the group of C.O.'s.

Phatmama's chest rose and fell; she was winded from stabbing the dog shit out of Jelli. All the pent up tension she had in her slowly started to seep from her body. Her thoughts returned to Boot. She missed him like nothing in the world mattered. She craved his touch, to see his smiling face. Tears welled up in her eyes. Phatmama walked over to Racks and wrapped her arms around Racks. She squeezed Racks tight, and Racks hugged her back while still pointing the gun at the sea of C.O.'s that was at the end of the tier. Phatmama kissed Racks' cheek. "I will see you on the other side," she mumbled in Racks' ear before she fished out the double shot derringer that was concealed in her panties. She put the tiny gun to her head and pulled the trigger, discharging both barrels, sending two 38 slugs into her brain. *Boom!* The gun echoed in *A Unit.*

Phatmama's body fell in slow motion. One of the females that witnessed Phatmama take her own life yelped. A C.O.

quickly ran through the crowd of C.O.'s. For the first time Racks noticed it was Ms. Flowers, better known to CTF as Big Freeda. Racks turned the pointing gun to her head. "Hold up, Ms. Banks!" a C.O. yelled, stepping out from the crowd of C.O.'s. Racks' finger rested on the trigger of the 380. She knew there was nothing that the C.O. could say to stop her from doing what her mind was set to do. But she heard him out anyway.

"Listen, young lady, I know things seem bad but they aren't that bad," the C.O. nervously said. He slowly walked towards Racks. "This is not the endgame of you. You don't have to end your story. There is still some good in you." The C.O. moved closer. "Please just give me the gun."

Racks' tears started falling and the C.O. knew he had Racks' attention; he had touched her heart. He moved closer. Racks dropped the gun to her waist and started crying uncontrollably. She quickly put the gun back to her head. The C.O. stopped in his tracks. "Come on, baby girl, please don't do this. Let's talk this situation out. I know you probably never had someone to hear your side of the story. But I'm here to listen, just put the gun down, sweetheart." The C.O. got close enough for Racks to read his name tag: Mobley. When Mobley was ten feet away from Racks, she turned the gun on him and cocked the hammer back on the gun. He froze.

"You want to hear my story, huh?" Racks asked through clenched jaws.

The way that Racks asked C.O. Mobley if he wanted to hear her story made a lump grow in his throat, and made it hard for him to swallow.

"Imagine being a boy trapped in a girl's body, trying to fit into this crazy place we call a world and maintain being normal in what they call life. Nothing was ever normal for me and

I never seem to fit in this fucked up place we call a world. The people judge too harsh and so unforgiving."

"But God forgives."

"Don't say shit to me about God!" Racks screamed. "Where the fuck was God when I was growing up with the rats and roaches, when me and my little cousin was starving. Tell me where the hell was God when Gene die, or when Zoey died. Where *the fuck was God* when them two niggas raped and violated me!" More tears came to Racks' face but she kept talking "Where was God when they told me that I was HIV positive. Empathy came to C.O. Mobley's eyes. He took a deep breath. Before he could speak, Racks asked another question. "Where is God now that I got this gun pointed at you? I will tell you God don't exist!" Racks pulled the trigger on the 380. *Boom!* C.O. Mobley was stuck in the middle of his head with a bullet. The C.O.'s at the top of the tier swiftly moved back at the unit, and the sally port door closed. Racks knew now that the SWAT team was probably on their way. Racks laid next to Phatmama on the floor and blew her brains out.

Jibril Williams

Chapter Thirty
Ninety Day Later

Tata walked out CTF a free woman. She smiled at Whip before she ran and jumped in his arms, wrapping her legs around his waist. She kissed him hard and shamelessly. Billie and Sticks watched. "I miss you so much, Papi!" Tata spoke and kissed Whip at the same time. She held on to Whip for what seemed like forever before she climbed out of Whip's arms, and hugged Sticks and Billie. Tata and Billie both had tears in their eyes.

"Billie, you know that you my top bitch now, right?" Tata said sincerely.

"And you know that I won't have it no other way," Billie stated through tears, affirming her status in Tata's life. Billie had turned herself in months ago for the warrant she had on her head for harboring a fugitive. It was conveyed to the courts that Billie didn't know Tata. She met her at Boot's repast. The defense argued that seeing Tata was drunk, Billie decided to do a good deed by giving her a ride home. They went for the story Billie gave them, and that was only because she was white, but the local police and the Feds questioned Billie. They asked her question about the robberies all the way to the incident with suicide murder at CTF. Billie denied every detail.

"Did you bring what I asked you?" Tata asked.

"Yeah, everything is ready," Billie replied.

Tata saw Kirby sitting in the passenger seat of Sticks' car. She rolled her eyes at him; she wanted to fuck him up so bad. But she knew he only did what Whip had ordered him to do. The hit on Jelli had happened a day before the actual plan. Everything they had planned—Kirby had gone back and told Whip. Whip didn't want Tata there doing the murder, so they choose to have her moved to another unit. Phatmama had dropped the note on Tata saying she feared for her safety, and Kirby dropped a note on Jelli and her being unsafe in B Unit. Kirby had found out that Meeka—the chick Jelli beat down with the soap in *A Unit*—was housed in *C Unit*. From working CTF he knew they would never put Jelli and Meeka in the same unit again because they had a fight, so there was only *A Unit* left for Jelli to go right into the arms of Phatmama and Racks. CTF only had three units to house female inmates—*A, B, C*. Kirby was the one who gave Phatmama and Racks access to the guns. That was no problem. He worked some big overtime in RD with Ms. Flowers, and he snuck the guns in through there. Even though Tata didn't like Kirby because he robbed her of the privilege to watch Jelli die, she had to be grateful.

"Listen, Whip, me and Billie have to do something."

"What you mean? You just got out. What the fuck you have to do?" Whip asked.

"I want to go to Phatmama and Racks' graves. I have to say my goodbyes, Whip." Whip could understand where Tata's head and heart was at. He knew Tata really loved those two women. He nodded.

"I will go with you," Whip stated.

"No, I want to do this with just me and Billie."

Whip paused and looked at Tata and then back at Billie. "You make sure she make it back to me in one hour," Whip said, pointing at Billie. He kissed Tata on the forehead.

"We got a party that's waiting on you—don't keep me waiting, baby," Whip said, getting into his car. Sticks pointed a finger at Billie and mouthed at her: "One hour." Billie just smiled at her lover. Billie got in her car and pulled off. "The bag is in the back seat," Billie said. Tata reached in the back seat and removed the bag. It was clothes in there. Tata stripped butt ass naked in Billie's car while they drove through traffic. "I'm sorry, girl but I just had to get them itchy ass panties off me," Tata said, throwing the CTF-issued panties out the window and sliding into a pair of boy shorts and then a black Prada jogging suit, and pushed her feet into a pair black air maxs.

"I got some loud pack," Billie offered.

"When we get done we can blow one," Tata said.

"Girl, I'm so glad that you are home, because I didn't know who was gonna walk me down the altar!"

"Altar? You getting married?" Tata asked, looking confused.

"Yup, Sticks' fine ass popped the question on me last month." Billie held up her hand and showed Tata her ring.

"Oh shit, Billie, I'm so happy for you, mami. When is the date?" Tata asked, showing she was really happy for Billie.

"In five months," Billie announced. "Oh—and that ain't all. I'm about to have a little Sticks running around here!" Billie stated.

"Bitch, stop playing. I know your ass ain't pregnant."

"Yes, I am. I'm two and half months," Billie confirmed.

"Wow!" Tata said, putting her hand on Billie's stomach.

"I know you letting me be the godmother so don't even play."

"Tata, you can be the godmother. Just promise me that you would love my baby like it's yours."

"I would die for your seed like it was mine," Tata said sincerely.

Billie nodded with respect to what Tata just said. Billie pulled her car into the Red Bottom lot parking lot. Tata stared at her pride and joy. All her hard work burned to the ground. But she held her composure. She wished she could have been behind the gun that killed Triple G. She didn't know the details of Triple G's death, but Whip assured her that Triple was taken care of and Spook was his new plug.

Tata and Billie got out the car. They used the club key to get in. The place smelt of charred wood. The fire damaged everything, and what the fire didn't damage the fire fighter water did from combating the fire. The ceiling had a hole in it, and birds and bats had already started making Club Red Bottomz their home.

"Tata, I told you shit wasn't here!"

"Just give me the bag with your pregnant ass and come on. Billie had already come to the club and took pics of the damage, but she didn't know why Tata wanted to come to the burned down club; it was a mystery to Billie. They stepped over broken boards and walked past smoke-stained walls. Tata stopped at the door of where her office used to be. The fire had reached her office but the office was as damaged as the rest of the club. Her desk was burned to ashes, and the floors of the office were weak as a result of the fire. Tata walked in and Billie slowly followed behind her, trying her best not to trip and fall.

Tata stopped at the burnt cabinet where her safe was stored. The fire had damaged the cabinet but when she opened it, the door creaked on its hinges. The safe in the cabinet was untouched by the fire. Tata smiled and looked over her shoulder at Billie. And it hit Billie that Tata's money was still in the safe. She was told by Whip that Tata had lost all her money in the club fire. He told how he had placed all Tata's money in the safe and in the drawer of her desk. Tata spun the dial of the safe with ease, and the safe door opened without a problem. The safe was packed with money. The safe would have withstood the fire anyway because it was fire proof. The fire fighters put the fire out before it really could destroy her office. Tata quickly put the money in the book bag and a few extra bags that Billie had inside the book bag. She then went over to the hundred-gallon fish tank. The piranhas that used to occupy the tank had died off. The murky waters were filled with the fish decay.

Tata removed a panel from the wall under the tank and turned a nob, and instantly the water started to drain." Billie and Tata watched as the water drained.

"Tata, what are you doing? You got your money, let's get the fuck outta here!" Billie stated.

"Just give me a few minutes," Tata stated, removing the gloves and small hammer Billie had packed in the book bag. She quickly put the gloves on and used the hammer to break the tank's glass. Tata used a glove hand to sift through the glass and fish tank gravel. Tata plucked a black diamond from the gravel and held it up in the air.

"Oh, you's a bad bitch!" Billie screamed. Tata plucked seven more diamonds from the gravel and put them in the pocket of her jogging suit.

"These are the diamonds for the Red Bottom Squad very first heist," Tata said. Billie's mouth went into a O shape with excitement in her eyes. Phatmama had told her about the heist.

"Let's go, Billie, take me to go see my girls," Tata mumbled.

Twenty-five minutes later, Tata stood over Phatmama and Boot's grave. They were buried next to each other. This was Tata's orders. Billie gave Tata some privacy and waited in the car. Tata wiped tears from her free. She missed the fuck outta Phatmama and Racks. The two fallen Red Bottom members gave the ultimate sacrifice. They killed Jelli and sacrificed their lives so she could walk as a free woman again. She will be forever grateful for her two friends; their names will end-lessly be part of her. Tata made plans to open a new club and name it after her fallen comrades. The club's name would be called Phat-Racks. Tata bent down and dropped four dia-monds apiece in a small hole she dug into Phatmama and Racks' grave. "These belong with you all," Tata said, filling the hole with dirt." I know you two are the two fliest ones in heaven. Kiss Zoey for me. I love you."

After those words, Tata walked away from Phatmama and Racks' graves. She was on to a new beginning. Life would never be the same without Phatmama, Zoey and Racks. She just hoped she could maintain without them.

The End

Lock Down Publications and Ca$h Presents assisted
publishing packages.

BASIC PACKAGE $499
Editing
Cover Design
Formatting

UPGRADED PACKAGE $800
Typing
Editing
Cover Design
Formatting

ADVANCE PACKAGE $1,200
Typing
Editing
Cover Design
Formatting
Copyright registration
Proofreading
Upload book to Amazon

LDP SUPREME PACKAGE $1,500
Typing
Editing
Cover Design
Formatting
Copyright registration
Proofreading
Set up Amazon account
Upload book to Amazon

Jibril Williams

Advertise on LDP Amazon and Facebook page

***Other services available upon request. Additional charges may apply
Lock Down Publications
P.O. Box 944
Stockbridge, GA 30281-9998
Phone # 470 303-9761

Submission Guideline

Submit the first three chapters of your completed manuscript to ldpsubmissions@gmail.com, subject line: Your book's title. The manuscript must be in a .doc file and sent as an attachment. Document should be in Times New Roman, double spaced and in size 12 font. Also, provide your synopsis and full contact information. If sending multiple submissions, they must each be in a separate email.

Have a story but no way to send it electronically? You can still submit to LDP/Ca$h Presents. Send in the first three chapters, written or typed, of your completed manuscript to:

LDP: Submissions Dept
Po Box 944
Stockbridge, Ga 30281

DO NOT send original manuscript. Must be a duplicate.

Provide your synopsis and a cover letter containing your full contact information.

Thanks for considering LDP and Ca$h Presents.

NEW RELEASES

TIL DEATH by ARYANNA
IT'S JUST ME AND YOU by AH'MILLION
QUEEN OF THE ZOO 2 by BLACK MIGO
THE HEART OF A SAVAGE 4 by JIBRIL WILLIAMS

By **T.J. Edwards**

GORILLAZ IN THE BAY V

3X KRAZY III

STRAIGHT BEAST MODE III

De'Kari

KINGPIN KILLAZ IV

STREET KINGS III

PAID IN BLOOD III

CARTEL KILLAZ IV

DOPE GODS III

Hood Rich

SINS OF A HUSTLA II

ASAD

RICH $AVAGE II

By Martell Troublesome Bolden

YAYO V

Bred In The Game 2

S. Allen

CREAM III

THE STREETS WILL TALK II

By Yolanda Moore

SON OF A DOPE FIEND III

HEAVEN GOT A GHETTO II

By Renta

LOYALTY AIN'T PROMISED III

By Keith Williams

I'M NOTHING WITHOUT HIS LOVE II

SINS OF A THUG II
TO THE THUG I LOVED BEFORE II
IN A HUSTLER I TRUST II
By Monet Dragun
QUIET MONEY IV
EXTENDED CLIP III
THUG LIFE IV
By **Trai'Quan**
THE STREETS MADE ME IV
By **Larry D. Wright**
IF YOU CROSS ME ONCE II
ANGEL IV
By **Anthony Fields**
THE STREETS WILL NEVER CLOSE IV
By K'ajji
HARD AND RUTHLESS III
KILLA KOUNTY III
By Khufu
MONEY GAME III
By Smoove Dolla
JACK BOYS VS DOPE BOYS II
A GANGSTA'S QUR'AN V
COKE GIRLZ II
By Romell Tukes
MURDA WAS THE CASE II
Elijah R. Freeman
THE STREETS NEVER LET GO II

By Robert Baptiste

AN UNFORESEEN LOVE III

By **Meesha**

KING OF THE TRENCHES III
by **GHOST & TRANAY ADAMS**

MONEY MAFIA II

LOYAL TO THE SOIL III

By **Jibril Williams**

QUEEN OF THE ZOO III

By **Black Migo**

VICIOUS LOYALTY III

By Kingpen

A GANGSTA'S PAIN III

By J-Blunt

CONFESSIONS OF A JACKBOY III

By Nicholas Lock

GRIMEY WAYS II

By Ray Vinci

KING KILLA II

By Vincent "Vitto" Holloway

BETRAYAL OF A THUG II

By Fre$h

THE MURDER QUEENS II

By Michael Gallon

THE BIRTH OF A GANGSTER II

By Delmont Player

TREAL LOVE II

By Le'Monica Jackson

FOR THE LOVE OF BLOOD II

By Jamel Mitchell

RAN OFF ON DA PLUG II

By Paper Boi Rari

HOOD CONSIGLIERE II

By Keese

PRETTY GIRLS DO NASTY THINGS II

By Nicole Goosby

PROTÉGÉ OF A LEGEND II

By Corey Robinson

IT'S JUST ME AND YOU II

By Ah'Million

Available Now

RESTRAINING ORDER **I & II**

By **CA$H & Coffee**

LOVE KNOWS NO BOUNDARIES **I II & III**

By **Coffee**

RAISED AS A GOON I, II, III & IV

BRED BY THE SLUMS I, II, III

BLAST FOR ME I & II

ROTTEN TO THE CORE I II III

Jibril Williams

A BRONX TALE I, II, III

DUFFLE BAG CARTEL I II III IV V VI

HEARTLESS GOON I II III IV V

A SAVAGE DOPEBOY I II

DRUG LORDS I II III

CUTTHROAT MAFIA I II

KING OF THE TRENCHES

By **Ghost**

LAY IT DOWN **I & II**

LAST OF A DYING BREED I II

BLOOD STAINS OF A SHOTTA I & II III

By **Jamaica**

LOYAL TO THE GAME I II III

LIFE OF SIN I, II III

By **TJ & Jelissa**

BLOODY COMMAS I & II

SKI MASK CARTEL I II & III

KING OF NEW YORK I II,III IV V

RISE TO POWER I II III

COKE KINGS I II III IV V

BORN HEARTLESS I II III IV

KING OF THE TRAP I II

By **T.J. Edwards**

IF LOVING HIM IS WRONG…I & II

LOVE ME EVEN WHEN IT HURTS I II III

By **Jelissa**

WHEN THE STREETS CLAP BACK I & II III

186

THE HEART OF A SAVAGE I II III IV

MONEY MAFIA

LOYAL TO THE SOIL I II

By **Jibril Williams**

A DISTINGUISHED THUG STOLE MY HEART I II & III

LOVE SHOULDN'T HURT I II III IV

RENEGADE BOYS I II III IV

PAID IN KARMA I II III

SAVAGE STORMS I II III

AN UNFORESEEN LOVE I II

By **Meesha**

A GANGSTER'S CODE I &, II III

A GANGSTER'S SYN I II III

THE SAVAGE LIFE I II III

CHAINED TO THE STREETS I II III

BLOOD ON THE MONEY I II III

A GANGSTA'S PAIN I II

By J-Blunt

PUSH IT TO THE LIMIT

By **Bre' Hayes**

BLOOD OF A BOSS **I, II, III, IV, V**

SHADOWS OF THE GAME

TRAP BASTARD

By **Askari**

THE STREETS BLEED MURDER **I, II & III**

THE HEART OF A GANGSTA I II& III

By **Jerry Jackson**

Jibril Williams

CUM FOR ME I II III IV V VI VII VIII

An **LDP Erotica Collaboration**

BRIDE OF A HUSTLA **I II & II**

THE FETTI GIRLS **I, II& III**

CORRUPTED BY A GANGSTA I, II III, IV

BLINDED BY HIS LOVE

THE PRICE YOU PAY FOR LOVE I, II ,III

DOPE GIRL MAGIC I II III

By **Destiny Skai**

WHEN A GOOD GIRL GOES BAD

By **Adrienne**

THE COST OF LOYALTY I II III

By **Kweli**

A GANGSTER'S REVENGE **I II III & IV**

THE BOSS MAN'S DAUGHTERS I II III IV V

A SAVAGE LOVE **I & II**

BAE BELONGS TO ME I II

A HUSTLER'S DECEIT I, II, III

WHAT BAD BITCHES DO I, II, III

SOUL OF A MONSTER I II III

KILL ZONE

A DOPE BOY'S QUEEN I II III

TIL DEATH

By **Aryanna**

A KINGPIN'S AMBITON

A KINGPIN'S AMBITION **II**

I MURDER FOR THE DOUGH

188

By **Ambitious**

TRUE SAVAGE I II III IV V VI VII

DOPE BOY MAGIC I, II, III

MIDNIGHT CARTEL I II III

CITY OF KINGZ I II

NIGHTMARE ON SILENT AVE

THE PLUG OF LIL MEXICO II

CLASSIC CITY

By **Chris Green**

A DOPEBOY'S PRAYER

By **Eddie "Wolf" Lee**

THE KING CARTEL **I, II & III**

By **Frank Gresham**

THESE NIGGAS AIN'T LOYAL **I, II & III**

By **Nikki Tee**

GANGSTA SHYT **I II &III**

By **CATO**

THE ULTIMATE BETRAYAL

By **Phoenix**

BOSS'N UP **I , II & III**

By **Royal Nicole**

I LOVE YOU TO DEATH

By **Destiny J**

I RIDE FOR MY HITTA

I STILL RIDE FOR MY HITTA

By **Misty Holt**

LOVE & CHASIN' PAPER

Jibril Williams

By **Qay Crockett**
TO DIE IN VAIN
SINS OF A HUSTLA
By **ASAD**
BROOKLYN HUSTLAZ
By **Boogsy Morina**
BROOKLYN ON LOCK I & II
By **Sonovia**
GANGSTA CITY
By **Teddy Duke**
A DRUG KING AND HIS DIAMOND I & II III
A DOPEMAN'S RICHES
HER MAN, MINE'S TOO I, II
CASH MONEY HO'S
THE WIFEY I USED TO BE I II
PRETTY GIRLS DO NASTY THINGS
By Nicole Goosby
TRAPHOUSE KING **I II & III**
KINGPIN KILLAZ I II III
STREET KINGS I II
PAID IN BLOOD **I II**
CARTEL KILLAZ I II III
DOPE GODS I II
By **Hood Rich**
LIPSTICK KILLAH **I, II, III**
CRIME OF PASSION I II & III
FRIEND OR FOE I II III

190

The Heart of a Savage 4

By **Mimi**

STEADY MOBBN' **I, II, III**

THE STREETS STAINED MY SOUL I II III

By **Marcellus Allen**

WHO SHOT YA **I, II, III**

SON OF A DOPE FIEND I II

HEAVEN GOT A GHETTO

Renta

GORILLAZ IN THE BAY **I II III IV**

TEARS OF A GANGSTA I II

3X KRAZY I II

STRAIGHT BEAST MODE I II

DE'KARI

TRIGGADALE I II III

MURDAROBER WAS THE CASE

Elijah R. Freeman

GOD BLESS THE TRAPPERS I, II, III

THESE SCANDALOUS STREETS I, II, III

FEAR MY GANGSTA I, II, III IV, V

THESE STREETS DON'T LOVE NOBODY I, II

BURY ME A G I, II, III, IV, V

A GANGSTA'S EMPIRE I, II, III, IV

THE DOPEMAN'S BODYGAURD I II

THE REALEST KILLAZ I II III

THE LAST OF THE OGS I II III

Tranay Adams

THE STREETS ARE CALLING

Duquie Wilson

MARRIED TO A BOSS I II III

By Destiny Skai & Chris Green

KINGZ OF THE GAME I II III IV V VI

Playa Ray

SLAUGHTER GANG I II III

RUTHLESS HEART I II III

By Willie Slaughter

FUK SHYT

By Blakk Diamond

DON'T F#CK WITH MY HEART I II

By Linnea

ADDICTED TO THE DRAMA I II III

IN THE ARM OF HIS BOSS II

By Jamila

YAYO I II III IV

A SHOOTER'S AMBITION I II

BRED IN THE GAME

By S. Allen

TRAP GOD I II III

RICH $AVAGE

MONEY IN THE GRAVE I II III

By Martell Troublesome Bolden

FOREVER GANGSTA

GLOCKS ON SATIN SHEETS I II

By Adrian Dulan

TOE TAGZ I II III IV

The Heart of a Savage 4

LEVELS TO THIS SHYT I II

IT'S JUST ME AND YOU

By Ah'Million

KINGPIN DREAMS I II III

RAN OFF ON DA PLUG

By Paper Boi Rari

CONFESSIONS OF A GANGSTA I II III IV

CONFESSIONS OF A JACKBOY I II

By Nicholas Lock

I'M NOTHING WITHOUT HIS LOVE

SINS OF A THUG

TO THE THUG I LOVED BEFORE

A GANGSTA SAVED XMAS

IN A HUSTLER I TRUST

By Monet Dragun

CAUGHT UP IN THE LIFE I II III

THE STREETS NEVER LET GO

By Robert Baptiste

NEW TO THE GAME I II III

MONEY, MURDER & MEMORIES I II III

By **Malik D. Rice**

LIFE OF A SAVAGE I II III

A GANGSTA'S QUR'AN I II III IV

MURDA SEASON I II III

GANGLAND CARTEL I II III

CHI'RAQ GANGSTAS I II III

KILLERS ON ELM STREET I II III

Jibril Williams

JACK BOYZ N DA BRONX I II III

A DOPEBOY'S DREAM I II III

JACK BOYS VS DOPE BOYS

COKE GIRLZ

By Romell Tukes

LOYALTY AIN'T PROMISED I II

By Keith Williams

QUIET MONEY I II III

THUG LIFE I II III

EXTENDED CLIP I II

By **Trai'Quan**

THE STREETS MADE ME I II III

By **Larry D. Wright**

THE ULTIMATE SACRIFICE I, II, III, IV, V, VI

KHADIFI

IF YOU CROSS ME ONCE

ANGEL I II III

IN THE BLINK OF AN EYE

By **Anthony Fields**

THE LIFE OF A HOOD STAR

By Ca$h & Rashia Wilson

THE STREETS WILL NEVER CLOSE I II III

By K'ajji

CREAM I II

THE STREETS WILL TALK

By Yolanda Moore

NIGHTMARES OF A HUSTLA I II III

By King Dream

CONCRETE KILLA I II III

VICIOUS LOYALTY I II

By Kingpen

HARD AND RUTHLESS I II

MOB TOWN 251

THE BILLIONAIRE BENTLEYS I II III

By Von Diesel

GHOST MOB

Stilloan Robinson

MOB TIES I II III IV V VI

By SayNoMore

BODYMORE MURDERLAND I II III

THE BIRTH OF A GANGSTER

By Delmont Player

FOR THE LOVE OF A BOSS

By C. D. Blue

MOBBED UP I II III IV

THE BRICK MAN I II III IV

THE COCAINE PRINCESS I II III IV V

By King Rio

KILLA KOUNTY I II III

By Khufu

MONEY GAME I II

By Smoove Dolla

A GANGSTA'S KARMA I II

By FLAME

Jibril Williams

KING OF THE TRENCHES I II

by **GHOST & TRANAY ADAMS**

QUEEN OF THE ZOO I II

By **Black Migo**

GRIMEY WAYS

By Ray Vinci

XMAS WITH AN ATL SHOOTER

By Ca$h & Destiny Skai

KING KILLA

By Vincent "Vitto" Holloway

BETRAYAL OF A THUG

By Fre$h

THE MURDER QUEENS

By Michael Gallon

TREAL LOVE

By Le'Monica Jackson

FOR THE LOVE OF BLOOD

By Jamel Mitchell

HOOD CONSIGLIERE

By Keese

PROTÉGÉ OF A LEGEND

By Corey Robinson

<u>BOOKS BY LDP'S CEO, CA$H</u>

TRUST IN NO MAN

TRUST IN NO MAN 2

TRUST IN NO MAN 3

BONDED BY BLOOD

SHORTY GOT A THUG

THUGS CRY

THUGS CRY 2

THUGS CRY 3

TRUST NO BITCH

TRUST NO BITCH 2

TRUST NO BITCH 3

TIL MY CASKET DROPS

RESTRAINING ORDER

RESTRAINING ORDER 2

IN LOVE WITH A CONVICT

LIFE OF A HOOD STAR

XMAS WITH AN ATL SHOOTER

Jibril Williams

CHANDLER PARK LIBRARY
12800 Harper Ave.
Detroit, MI 48213